The World that Was

A Haunting Dystopian Tale

Book 2

∞

Heather Carson

Table of Contents

[Chapter 1](#)

[Chapter 2](#)

[Chapter 3](#)

[Chapter 4](#)

[Chapter 5](#)

[Chapter 6](#)

[Chapter 7](#)

[Chapter 8](#)

[Chapter 9](#)

[Chapter 10](#)

[Chapter 11](#)

[Chapter 12](#)

[Chapter 13](#)

[Chapter 14](#)

[Chapter 15](#)

[Chapter 16](#)

[Chapter 17](#)

[Chapter 18](#)

[Chapter 19](#)

All Rights Reserved.

Copyright © 2020 Heather Carson

Courtesy of Blue Tuesday Books

Cover Design by Fay Lane at faylane.com

ISBN: 9798652329129

Chapter 1

∞

The morning sun burned my eyes as I drove down the desert road. Brayson slept fitfully against the passenger side window, jerking awake at every bump. I tried to maneuver the truck slowly to avoid the potholes and washed out ruts of the highway.

Crumbling trailers and small broken-down trading outposts that we passed along the way were haunting reminders of the past. The world around us hung in a suspended state of decay. Giant letters from a sign that once said "gas station" had fallen onto the road. I turned the wheel and carefully drove around them. Every bit of the scenery we'd seen that day reminded me of a surreal fantasy book.

I loved it. We hadn't seen another living soul the entire trip. There was a part of me that was sad my ideal small town waiting to welcome us with open arms was just a fairy tale. Now that we were out of the city, I saw the vast emptiness of the world. There was truly no one left out here, just miles of abandoned buildings nestled into pockets of desert wasteland. I'd never felt so free.

And lost...

"Brayson, wake up. I think I took a wrong turn somewhere." The sun was now reflecting off the side mirrors. I vaguely recalled learning somewhere this meant I was heading west.

"How long was I out?" Brayson was suddenly alert beside me.

"I'm not sure." I pulled the truck off the road and opened the map, embarrassed to admit I was daydreaming and couldn't remember how long I'd been driving this road. "There was a highway marker a few miles back that had fallen halfway from the sign. I thought I turned on the right road, but now I'm not so sure."

"You shouldn't have turned off Hwy 93 at all. Where was this turn?" He leaned over and checked the lines I was pointing to.

"It was at this 229/93 split thingy." I glared at the top of his head. "You do realize I've never been more than twenty miles outside of LA, right?"

"You think I've been all over the world?" Brayson snapped.

"Well you've been farther away than I have." I shoved the map into his arms. "You and your fancy job outside the city." Brayson rolled his eyes and then looked to the gas gauge.

"Fawn." His voice was serious and condescending. "I told you to wake me up when you got to a quarter of a tank."

I glanced down at the needle. *Crap, he did tell me to do that.*

"Wake up. Gas is one quarter of a tank." I opened the truck door and slammed it behind me as I stepped out onto the road. Overgrown sagebrush as tall as my hips ate the edges of the asphalt and other weeds broke through the cracks of the pavement. I leaned against the hot metal of the vehicle and took a couple of deep breaths. The air felt so different out here.

A few minutes later, Brayson stepped out to join me.

"Look at those mountains." I pointed straight ahead. "Is that Idaho?"

He held up the map. "No. I think those are the Ruby Mountains. We are still in Nevada."

"Okay. Well let's turn around and head back to the main road."

"We don't have very much gas left. I wish I'd grabbed another can." Brayson's eyes were red from the lack of sleep. Or maybe it was from the weight of everything.

I lowered my voice. "What should we do?"

"I don't know." He ran a hand through his hair. "I just know we aren't making it to Idaho."

I instantly felt awful about everything. Burning down The Nocere, leaving everyone behind, asking Brayson to steal the blueprints- this was all my fault. Vorie was dead because of me. I missed Genie and I knew she would be mad at me for a long time. That is, if I ever got to see her again.

And Alister? I forced myself to push the image of his face deep down in my memories. I barely even knew him, but a part of me was drawn to him in a way I couldn't explain. I knew Roger said not to tell anyone the name of who killed him, but Alister seemed so worried maybe he should know. *He said he'd be right back…*

I'd ruined that too probably, and there was nothing I could do about the mess of a life I'd somehow created in the blink of an eye.

"I'm sorry you had to come with me," I whispered.

Brayson smirked. "Don't be. It's not your fault. Vorie wouldn't have let me live in this world or the next if I had abandoned you."

Thinking of Vorie scolding him with her sweet voice made me smile. "You know, she would have thought the Ruby Mountains sounded cool. Why don't we go check them out? Idaho isn't going anywhere any time soon."

"Alright," Brayson sighed. "But I'm driving so we don't get lost again."

Chapter 2

∞

We followed the highway up the mountain, and then turned down an overgrown dirt road with a campsite marker on it. Where the road ended in a thicket of trees, there was a small building buried in younger branches. Brayson parked the truck.

"This place look okay?" he asked.

"Let's check it out." Despite everything that had happened, I'd be lying if I said I wasn't overly excited. As soon as I opened the door, I heard the sound of rushing water.

"Brayson," I turned to him wide eyed. "I think there is a river here." I'd never seen a real river. I scrambled out of the truck with Brayson calling after me to slow down. Then I crashed through the brush until I found the source of the noise.

Waves of water clear as ice rippled away on the rocks in front of me. "Wow," I said. "I thought rivers were bigger for some reason."

Brayson came up behind me. "I think this is considered a creek not a river," he said.

"Hmm." I tried to stretch my neck out so I could see past the bushes to where the water was coming from. I slipped on the muddy bank. My knees caught my fall and my hands splashed into the creek.

"It's freezing," I laughed, pushing my hand into the water again. I could feel the current tug against my skin. To my right was a shallow pool carved out by dark purple rocks. Something silver drifted lazily in a circle.

"There are fish in here!" I screamed. The silver little thing quickly darted away down the stream.

"There might be," Brayson smiled. "If you don't scare them all away first."

We left the water and made our way back to the truck. Brayson and I began snapping away the branches so we could check out the hidden building. It was a small shack with two doors side by side. We cleared the debris from the cement porch in front of one heavy metal door and pulled it open.

Dusty air and cobwebs smacked us in the face as we peered inside. Yellow light filtered through a tiny stained window high in the corner, illuminating a single toilet, metal trash can, porcelain sink, and mirror. It was a large room to contain so little. Brayson quickly cleared the path to the second door and exposed a duplicate room like the first.

"Well," I said, taking a step back to inspect the building. "I guess we found the bathrooms."

"I wonder if the pipes still work?" Brayson emptied a bucket from the back of the truck and filled it with water from the creek. Then he poured the bucket into the toilet tank. We both held our breath as he flushed it. It worked.

"Look at that." I nudged him smiling. "Indoor plumbing."

The area around the restrooms was overgrown, but the main road provided a small walkway. We surveyed the area. There were no other structures. We did find a few picnic tables rotting away, but nothing we could use.

"Guess we are sleeping in the bathrooms," Brayson shrugged.

"Our very own private rooms," I mumbled.

Using a pine branch with short needles, I brushed out the cobwebs and swept the floor of my new home. Then we filled the buckets with more creek water and my fingers froze as I did my best to scrub the sink and toilet. Brayson started unloading boxes from the truck.

The boxes contained mostly canned food, so we split them up equally to not use all the space in a single room. Brayson silently handed me a sleeping bag and Vorie's winter clothes. I hugged them to my chest and cried once I walked into my room.

She never got to wear them and now she never would.

I stacked the farming books she'd given me on a box I'd designated as my shelf. Then I unrolled the sleeping bag. The room felt smaller with everything in there, but it would have to do.

We started a fire in one of the metal trashcans and set a pot to boil of rice with canned chicken. The sun was beginning to set. We scooted closer to the fire while clutching our flashlights as the food finished cooking.

"Next time we should start this earlier," I yawned. "I didn't realize how much longer it takes to cook over an open fire."

"Now we know," Brayson said stoically. "I'm sure we'll learn a lot of things as we go." A high pitched almost screeching yip sounded from off in the distance.

"What the hell is that?" I whispered as I grabbed his shirt sleeve. We shined our flashlights into the woods, but nothing moved.

"Probably just a wild animal," he concluded.

"Can we work on learning how to shoot the gun tomorrow?" I giggled nervously.

*

I was exhausted as I climbed into my sleeping bag for the night. It'd been two days since I'd gotten any real sleep. It's amazing how things can change in such a short period of time. A week ago, I was in the realm celebrating Genie's end of service at Dives. Alister had whisked me away for a moment. The details of his face and those bright green eyes staring at me on the pier of his manifestation…

Yeah, but that night at Dives was the night Vorie died, I reminded myself. *Not the greatest memory to have at all.*

I drifted in and out of sleep having nightmares of the monster who'd almost got me as a child and instead killed my friend. Part of me wished I would have turned around to watch him burn. The fire in my dreams kept dying out. I woke up with my teeth chattering.

The floor was so cold I could feel it in my bones. I flicked on my flashlight and pushed open the metal door, cringing at the loud noise it made. It was the middle of the night and I didn't want to wake Brayson up. He hadn't slept well the past few days either.

I grabbed my sleeping bag and dragged it to the truck, tripping on a root in the dark. As soon as I climbed into the cab, I heard Brayson's snores coming from the driver side. He'd leaned the bucket seat as far back as it would go and didn't stir once as I pushed my seat back too.

*

I opened the door and the cool morning air slapped me in the face. Groaning as I untangled myself from the sleeping bag, I slowly climbed out of the truck. The sun was peeking through the trees. I heard little chirps of music notes all around me. It was jarring, and I unconsciously reached up to turn my earbuds off. My hand lingered on my knotted hair as I remembered I'd left them behind.

I spun around in circles trying to find where the music was coming from. A movement on one of the branches above caught my eye. *There were birds!* Chirping, singing little birds fluttering on top of the trees in the early morning light.

"Brayson, do you hear this?" I reached across the inside of the cab and shook him. "Wake up dude and listen." His eyes came into focus as he strained to hear the sound. A smile briefly lit up his face before being replaced with a pained expression.

"They are just birds." He pulled the sleeping bag up to his chin and turned away from me.

"Have you ever seen a bird before?" I stared hard at his back willing him to get up.

"Yes," he mumbled. "There are seagulls on the beach sometimes."

"You've been to the beach before?" I kept probing him.

"Yeah. I took Vorie a few times," he said quietly. Sadness tainted with jealousy washed over me. I didn't know Vorie had seen the beach.

"Close the door Fawn. It's cold."

"Are you going to sleep all day?" I crossed my arms.

"Why not?" Brayson sighed. "It's not like we have anything better to do."

I slammed the door as loudly as I could and made my way down to the creek with a bucket.

Chapter 3

∞

My plan was to carry some water back up to my room, but when I saw the crystal-clear flowing stream, I left the bucket on the bank. The water was freezing as I splashed handfuls of it onto my face to wash the sleep from my eyes. Then I got the bright idea to strip naked and bathe in the cool water. *It wasn't the smartest plan I ever had.*

The birds and bugs danced on the water's edge. I stood shivering in the creek as I washed the dried blood from my arm. The wound from where I cut out my tracker was scabbing over. It was a small price to pay so that those jerks would never find me.

After squealing and screaming as I hurriedly finished washing the rest of my body, I climbed on top of a large rock and sat in the sun to dry. My teeth were chattering but the bath was invigorating. After pulling my wet hair into a bun and getting dressed, I filled the bucket of water to carry back to the truck.

"Go away," Brayson moaned as I opened the driver side door. He got a handful of cold creek water splashed in his face.

"What the hell?" he screamed as he bolted upright.

"I miss her too." I readied another handful of water and he scooted back against the center console. "But this isn't living and Vorie would want us to live. We'll see her again, I can promise you that, but I can't let you mope around for the rest of your life. Listen to the birds, man. Wake up. We've got work to do. Real work."

Brayson put his arm over his face as I splashed more water on him. "Fine. I'm up. You're an ass."

"Eh," I shrugged. "I don't mean to be."

*

We spent the morning making oatmeal over the fire and cutting down tiny aspen trees. Brayson worked to fix the trees into small cots to get us up off the concrete floors at night. They weren't pretty, but they held our weight.

In the afternoon, we walked a short distance down the road to a clearing in the trees.

"There's twenty bullets in this box," Brayson counted. "We can each practice with four and that leaves us twelve for an emergency." A dark cloud passed over the sun. "If the mafia comes, they'll bring more than twelve people."

I shook my head. "If the mafia comes, we wouldn't be able to shoot them all anyway. Don't worry about that, they won't find us with no trackers, and the great thing about the wild is there are no other people around." It took a lot of tinkering, but we finally figured out how to load the magazine.

"There's a safety switch," I said proudly.

"How do you know that?"

"I read it in a murder mystery book."

"Well where is it at?"

"That I don't know." Luckily, it was easy to find.

We laughed as we put the gun away and walked back home to start dinner, teasing each other about who was the worse shot the whole time.

A few minutes after we settled into our rooms for the night, I heard a loud *snap* followed by the sound of Brayson cursing.

"The damn cot broke," he yelled in frustration. "I'll fix it in the morning. I'm sleeping in the truck." I stifled a giggle with my sweater sleeve as I heard his boots stomping past my door.

*

Mary had a little lamb…

The soothing voice tugged me out of my nightmarish dreams. I laid there on the cot, wrapped in my warm sleeping bag, as the air around my face grew instantly colder.

Little lamb...

I wasn't sure if I was still asleep. I sat up quickly to check and the cot rocked from my movement but held firm.

Its fleece was white as snow...

"Vorie is that you?" I was definitely awake. The flashlight was on the box near my head. I grabbed it and almost dropped it as I quickly turned on the beam. No one else was in the room.

"This isn't funny. I swear I heard you." The light bounced along the walls as I checked all four corners again. Sighing, I clicked off the light and laid back down on the bed. *Going crazy is exactly what I need right now.* I closed my eyes and tried to go back to sleep.

"Boo."

"Damn it Vorie! That is not cool. You scared the crap out of me." I turned my head to the side to see the translucent outline of my friend's face laying on the jacket pillow next to me.

"Keep it down," she giggled. "You'll wake the dead."

"Always with the jokes," I groaned, but was still smiling. "So, you made it? You crossed over and you're safe in the realm? Brayson is going to be so happy to hear this."

"Shh." Vorie's voice was different. More melodic and distant than in real life. It gave me goosebumps. "I don't want him to know that I came to see you yet. He'll be hurt."

"Not if you go see him too. He is over there in the truck," I laughed. "He built these cots and his broke."

"I know." Her voice was so sad that I instantly felt like the worst friend ever. "But he isn't ready to see me yet. His soul is still reaching for the realm right now and I don't think it's a good idea to tip the scales. Plus, I'm still learning how to do this thing and I'm not sure how long I can stay."

"What's it like?" I asked. "Traveling back to the real world."

"Different," Vorie smiled. "The complete opposite of going through the portals. No darkness, the void is light, but it's hard to ground myself here in this world. In this…" she giggled as she looked over my head. "This bathroom. Was this seriously the best place you could find?"

"Hey." I stuck out my bottom lip. "I cleaned it all up and I happen to think it is very cozy." Vorie chuckled.

"I have to go now," she said suddenly. "I just came to tell you that something is coming. You don't need to run away or be afraid. Just be prepared and trust your gut."

"Um, that's a little ominous. Care to elaborate?"

Vorie shook her head sadly. "Take care of Brayson for me."

"Wait," I reached out to grab her, but my hand slipped through. "I saw birds today. They were singing."

Her essence disappeared, but her words lingered in the room. "I saw them with you."

*

Brayson and I worked together after breakfast to reinforce his cot.

"We should probably figure out how to eat some of the stuff around here," I said as I opened another can of sausages. "The food we brought isn't going to last us forever." Brayson murmured something inaudible while he fastened a rope around the wood to secure the corner.

"I'm going to assume that was "yes Fawn, I agree." Great. Let's figure out a way to get us some fish." I caught the slightest hint of a smile on his face before he looked to the ground.

*

After searching through the supplies to discover we didn't have any hooks or fishing poles, I was standing in the creek trying to figure out how to turn a t-shirt into a net. Suddenly, I heard the sound of approaching engines.

"Brayson!" I screamed as I crashed through the bushes while running up the hill. "I think someone's coming!"

He stood in the clearing by the truck with his hands in the air. The pistol was on the ground a few feet away from his feet.

"Walk out slowly Fawn and cover your arm," he whispered loud enough for me to hear.

I pulled the sleeves of my sweater down and inched my way over to his side. There were six ATVs forming a half circle around us blocking the road. The riders held long guns pointed at our heads.

"Who are they?" I asked without moving my lips while raising my hands in the air.

The riders looked worn down with dirty faces. Some wore cowboy hats or bandannas, but most of them were wearing jeans and t-shirts. I'd never seen anyone in the mafia dress like that. My heart was racing, but Vorie's words gave me a small bit of comfort.

A dirt bike came roaring through the center of their formation. The new rider dismounted and removed her helmet, exposing a cascade of long black hair. She reminded me of Astrid, and I felt another twinge of the guilt that plagued me for leaving my coworkers too.

The woman motioned for one of the ATV riders to go check the bathroom structure. Brayson stepped forward protectively and she raised her hand.

"We're not here to take your stuff." She sounded annoyed. "I just want to make sure there are no hidden surprises coming my way." The man calmly returned from his inspection of our rooms and whispered something into her ear.

The woman turned her sharp eyes toward us and smirked. "Walk over here with your hands up. I'd tell you to stay away from the gun, but Akon over here says you can't shoot for shit." The man to the right of me chuckled. I felt my cheeks grow hot.

"And you are living in the bathrooms." The woman shook her head and set her helmet on the handlebar. "Want to tell me what the hell you two are doing out here?"

Brayson stepped forward again. "We didn't mean to infringe on anyone's turf. We were just looking to leave the city and make a life for ourselves in the wild."

"Sure you were," the woman laughed. "Who are you running from?" Brayson's eyes locked with mine as he glanced back over his shoulder.

"He's telling the truth," I said coldly. I was seriously starting to dislike this lady. "Where we come from is trash. There's no jobs, no wildlife. There is nothing there except portals. We wanted to get as far away from all that as we could. It was always our plan to leave once we turned eighteen and our contracts were up." I omitted the rest, hoping she wouldn't see through the lie.

"You're orphans?" she asked in a sympathetic tone which was quickly replaced by sarcasm. "They sure don't teach you anything, do they? The supplies you have will barely last you through the summer. You'll freeze to death up here this winter. Do you plan on moving before then? The last thing I want to do is shoot a couple of starving kids trying to raid my town."

"We don't have enough gas to go anywhere," Brayson sighed. "But I promise we won't be a problem."

"Of course, you're stuck here." The woman let out an exasperated huff as she looked to the sky. "Get them some gas, will you Roger? You kids pack up your gear and follow me back to the village." Roger pulled a gas tank from the back of his ATV and walked over to fill the truck.

"Thank you for the gas," I said, standing firmly where I was. "But we will be okay up here. I can give you some cans of beans in exchange for the fuel."

The woman laughed. "I'm not taking your food and I'm not asking. You two will come down to the village. We'll put you to work in exchange for teaching you some skills. If you choose to leave after that's up to you, but your blood won't be on my hands then."

Brayson turned to me with pleading eyes. I reluctantly nodded and dragged my feet as we both moved to load up our belongings. The other ATV riders left, and the woman waited by her bike until we put the last box in the back.

"What are your names?" she asked before we got into the truck.

"Fawn and Brayson. What's yours?"

"Juniper." She looked down at my long sleeve. "Show me your trackers." I bit my lip and avoided her gaze. "That's what I thought. Don't tell anyone in my village. I don't want them scared that you might be bringing trouble."

"Thank you for doing this," Brayson said.

"Don't thank me yet," Juniper laughed as she put on her helmet.

Chapter 4

∞

The road leading down the other side of the mountain was eroded and hard to travel in the truck. The grated dirt road Juniper turned onto was much smoother than the broken asphalt. Through the dust she kicked up from her bike, we saw rows of rusted trailers with tarps and tents extending out from their sides.

Barefoot, dirty children ran into the yards and waved as we passed by. A few older boys chased the truck with a stick until a woman wearing a faded yellow apron and waving a threatening spoon called them back inside.

"It's so alive," I gasped as I turned to wave at the kids through our back window.

"I don't know if you can call this living," Brayson said. "It looks like a hard life. There is nothing here. It's all desert. Why don't they move up to the mountain?"

Past the trailers was a small town boasting a handful of rundown business structures. Juniper dropped her kickstand in front of a decaying building with the word "HOTEL" stamped on the front. She walked inside without waiting for us. We stood awkwardly on the sidewalk, leaning against the truck.

"Here," she said after she came out a few minutes later and placed a key in my hand. "There's a town meeting tonight at the courthouse down the street. Be there at six."

"How can we pay you?" Brayson asked. I slid my arm behind my back, suddenly very aware that we didn't have currency to live in the real world. Juniper noticed the movement.

"Don't worry about that. We don't use credits here. You'll work for what you get." She fixed the helmet onto her head and jumped back on her bike.

*

Inside the dusty old hotel lobby sat an ancient woman with deep wrinkles creasing her face.

"Welcome," she smiled with missing teeth. "I'm Mrs. Shaw. Your room is just up the stairs. Dinner is normally at six, but with the meeting tonight I'll have it ready by five. Come on down to the kitchen once you've unpacked."

We lugged our boxes up the single flight of stairs. The room was wallpapered in fading orange and brown strips. There was a simple burgundy sofa in the main sitting area and a small table with chairs that sat below a window overlooking the main street. A single bed, dresser, and nightstand were tucked away in the side room behind French doors.

"This isn't that bad," I said while kicking the entrance door closed behind me.

"I'll sleep on the couch." Brayson dropped his stack of boxes in the corner.

"That's not fair." I reached for the door handle. "I'll go ask Mrs. Shaw if we can get a second room."

"Leave it Fawn." Brayson sat on the sofa and closed his eyes. "I don't know how much debt we are already racking up. Until they tell us how we are supposed to pay it back, I don't want to add any more."

The scent of cooking food wafted up the stairs. My stomach rumbled. It'd been a few days since we'd eaten anything that smelled that good. I pulled Brayson down the stairs and into the kitchen.

A large table set for five took up half the room. Mrs. Shaw carried over a plate stacked high with brown crinkled rocks and placed it on the table. A man about the same ancient age as Mrs. Shaw carried over a steaming tray of meat from the oven.

"Smells delicious sweetheart." Mr. Shaw grinned at his wife and she swatted him with a dishcloth.

"Go fetch Olie and tell her dinner is ready," she instructed him.

Oleen was a freckled little girl about twelve years old. *I can't believe that's how young I was the first time I was sent to the realm.* She came running in from the back alley when Mr. Shaw called her name.

Brayson and I stood transfixed watching the homely scene. This didn't exist in the world we grew up in and I felt like an intruder to their happiness.

"Come eat." Mrs. Shaw pushed us toward the table. We took our seats quietly and waited for the tray of meat to get passed around. When Mr. Shaw and Oleen grabbed the brown rocks, I eyed them skeptically. Oleen cut open one of them with a fork and smeared a yellow cream over the steaming inside.

I didn't want to seem rude, so I grabbed a rock for my plate. It wasn't as firm as I imagined it would be and it was hot enough to burn my fingers. I copied what Oleen had done with the yellow spread. After it melted into the white fluffy inside, I scooped out a tentative bite.

"It's like potatoes," I exclaimed, and instantly covered my mouth.

"It is potatoes." Mr. Shaw raised an eyebrow at me. Brayson quickly handed over the meat dish and I spooned some onto my plate.

"What kind of meat is this?" Brayson asked as he took another bite.

"Venison and gravy." Mrs. Shaw held her fork midair as she studied us. "Where are you two from?"

I swallowed my spoonful of meat. It was different than the canned meat. Richer, less salty, almost pungent. "The city. Down south."

The Shaws muttered a simultaneous "ah" and continued to eat their food. After dinner, I helped Mrs. Shaw clear away the dishes.

"Where do you get real potatoes?" I couldn't help but ask. "We can sometimes find the boxed kind, but I've never seen real ones before."

Mrs. Shaw looked at me like I had two heads. "The box kind is just a dehydration of the real kind, but Fallon grows potatoes and sells them at his market."

"Oh," I nodded, hoping to brush off my ignorance.

"Where are your parents, girl?" Mrs. Shaw crossed her skinny arms over her chest.

"I don't know," I shrugged. "I'm an orphan. So is Brayson. So is pretty much everyone I know."

"I see," Mrs. Shaw said sadly. "That's why Juniper must have brought you here. She was an orphan many years ago. No matter now. Leave the dishes and go get ready for the meeting."

*

The courthouse looked as if it had been gutted a long time ago. The main room now held a bunch of mismatched chairs facing a long bench desk. Men and women with dirt lined faces filled the chairs and talked in hushed tones as they waited for the meeting to begin.

It was odd to see so many people gathered in one place without the use of glamour. A few of them glanced at us as Brayson and I took a seat near the back. The commotion in the room settled as two men and Juniper took the seats at the desk.

"The monthly community meeting will begin. The proceedings will follow standard protocol and the floor will be open for discussion in a few minutes." The man to the right of Juniper shuffled some pages as he spoke.

"As we all know, the government has been sending what they call "relief packages" along with representatives in order to incorporate our village into part of their country. We've continued to refuse them at the decision of this consul as we wish to remain free from their control. Considering the seclusion of our area, and the limited amount of resources this so-called government possesses, we don't feel this will be an issue for our community. In keeping with procedure, we put this decision once again to vote. All those in favor of remaining a sovereign community say aye."

The room erupted with what sounded like a unanimous aye.

The speaker sighed loudly. "Opposed. Say nay."

A single voice from the middle of the crowd said, "nay."

"Give it a rest will you, Theo," a woman sitting near me said. There were groans from others in the room.

"Let him speak," the man to the left of Juniper said as he cast her a long look. "You all know the rules. Majority wins but minority is given a voice."

"It's the same thing every time," the woman sitting next to me muttered under her breath.

Theo stood up. He was young with a perfectly trimmed beard and a clean flannel checkered shirt. It contrasted sharply with the faded clothes in the rest of the room.

"I wish you all would at least consider it," Theo said. "If the government wants to help and they are giving free stuff, why not let them? They won't be able to do anything to change our way of life, but they might provide us with some protection if the mafia ever returns."

"Boy, sit down," an old man grunted from his seat in the front row. "You were a child the last time the mafia came here. We don't have anything they want. None of us frequent the realm that often, but they come every decade or so to offer us trackers. We send them packing every time they come." An easy smile came to my face at the man's words.

"And nothing comes without a price. You're too young to remember what a centralized government was," the elderly woman sitting beside him glared up at Theo. "But some of us don't ever want to see that again." Theo folded his arms across his chest as he sat back down in his seat.

"Moving on," the man at the desk continued, "We are taking a vote today to move the marketplace to the town center. Fallon and Mazier have agreed to a slight increase of the price of their goods to cover the fuel cost of transport from their farms to here. This will help offset the travel cost of the consumers. Market days will remain Saturday. All those in favor, say aye." No one disagreed.

"Final order of business. The eastern slope of the mountain range has been showing a decline in wildlife. The council recommends avoiding hunting in this section to allow regrowth of the population. The Northwest region should be the area to utilize for the remainder of the year. In favor?" The room unanimously agreed.

"Before we open the floor," Juniper said as the man to her left opened a notebook. "I have one more topic. The young adults Akon found while documenting the ridge have been brought into town."

I shifted uneasily on the chair as Brayson stiffened beside me.

"They finished their indentured servitude to the mafia and left the city to live free in the wild. Unfortunately, they lack the skills to do that. I brought them here to learn from you in exchange for any work you can give. Do you agree with this plan?"

All the eyes in the room turned toward Brayson and me. My hands were clammy as I wrung them in my lap. I looked to Juniper in confusion. *Why would she make us come here just to cast us out?*

"Aye," the sound coursed through the room. A woman near me smiled warmly and a man reached over to clap Brayson on the back.

The floor opened for discussion as people stood to give grievances or offer suggestions. My heart was still pounding from the embarrassment of the vote long after the meeting was adjourned. I caught Juniper as she was walking out the door and pulled her to the side.

"What if they said no?" I asked her.

"They wouldn't have." She took my hand off her sleeve and stared into my eyes. "We vote on everything here, but I wouldn't have brought you if I knew they'd say no. That's the benefit of living with likeminded individuals." Juniper walked off down the darkened street to her waiting bike.

"I feel like you shouldn't piss her off," Brayson scolded as we walked down the sidewalk to the hotel.

"Yeah. I get that feeling too."

Chapter 5

∞

We were awake early the next morning and stood in the hotel lobby unsure of what to do with ourselves.

"Go stack the firewood in the back lot and fill the boxes," Mrs. Shaw directed Brayson. She handed me a bucket full of water and soap. "You start washing the front walls. Breakfast is in an hour."

We rushed through the morning chores and hurried to join the family at the table. There were real eggs and fresh baked bread to eat.

"I'll have more for you to do this evening so you can earn your stay here," Mrs. Shaw said as she pushed us out the door. "But Juniper wants you two at the farm to meet Fallon."

Brayson drove the truck down the unfamiliar roads as I read the directions hastily scribbled on a piece of paper.

"This is so amazing." I couldn't stop staring at the landscape and smiling at all the people we passed. "We are going to an actual farm and we ate real freaking eggs for breakfast. Tell me those weren't the most delicious things you've ever had."

Brayson looked sullenly out the window as he drove. "They were alright."

"Come on. None of this is interesting to you at all?" I hadn't noticed his mood until now and had to backtrack down from my excitement.

"Vorie would have loved this," he whispered.

"Vorie wants you to be happy. You know that, and you know you'll see her again soon." I bit my lip so I wouldn't say anymore. Brayson just nodded.

We pulled up to the farm and Fallon came out to greet us. He was a fast-moving man with a wad of tobacco in his front lip which he spit constantly on the ground. With the market moving to the town center on the weekend, he needed extra help to harvest produce which was normally picked by the customers.

Fallon talked nonstop as he worked and answered all the questions I threw at him with enthusiasm. He kept us moving all day long, directing our movements with a nudge and a point, never breaking his stream of conversation.

My arms were shaking and sore as we climbed into the truck for the drive back to the hotel. Between Fallon's chatter, the farm labor, and our chores, we were too exhausted to do more than fall asleep after dinner the first few days.

Midweek things started to get easier. I don't know if we hit our stride or if they loosened the reins a bit for us. By market day, even Brayson was more talkative.

*

We sat at the table that Saturday morning helping ourselves to stacks of Mrs. Shaw's apple cinnamon pancakes. Brayson stole the syrup jar out of my hands and I pouted dramatically until he gave it back. Oleen began to giggle uncontrollably which sent us all into a fit of laughter.

"Where'd you two meet?" Mr. Shaw asked, wiping the happy tears off his cheek. The light in Brayson's eyes faltered.

I smiled at him warmly before turning to Mr. Shaw. "We kind of knew each other at the orphanage, but it wasn't until he started dating my best friend that we got close." Mrs. Shaw put her hand over her mouth in indignation.

"Nothing like that," I reassured her quickly. "We are just friends. Vorie, my best friend and Brayson's fiancé, passed away a little while ago. I guess her death accelerated the move we'd been planning for so long."

"Oh dear." Mrs. Shaw dropped her hand to her lap. "I'm so sorry for your loss. You should have said something. We assumed you were a couple, so I put you in the same room."

"Brayson's been sleeping on the couch." I playfully bumped his shoulder with mine.

"That won't do at all." Mrs. Shaw rushed to the front room and came back with a key. "You move your stuff to the room across the hall," she told him.

"Are you sure ma'am?" Brayson looked to his plate. "We don't want to intrude any more than we already have."

"Nonsense." She grabbed his hand and thrust the key into it. "You two have been an enormous help. We were a little worried at first, seeing as though you are city folks, but you haven't stopped working since you got here. You've earned a bed to sleep on." Brayson smiled gratefully at her.

"What was it like in the orphanage?" Oleen asked.

"As long as Vorie was there it was good," I laughed. We told the Shaws all about Vorie during the rest of breakfast and the sag in Brayson's shoulders lifted a little bit.

*

The town's main street was transformed from a dusty road into a flurry of activity and excitement. Kids ran laughing down the street weaving in and out of the stands. Fallon waved us over to help unpack the crates of produce. He introduced us to Mazier who he described as his arch nemesis. The two men joked and laughed between their stalls the whole day.

Other smaller stands were set up by some of the locals displaying various wares for sale. Hand stitched clothing, jars of honey, bars of soap, and bags of dried meats filled the market stalls.

Brayson stopped to look at the clothing. "Why would anyone buy this?" he whispered once we were out of earshot. "They can get this for free from the stuff left behind in the big stores."

"I don't think there are any big stores around here," I laughed. "But it seems to be a self-sufficiency thing. The real question is why did they wait so long to do this? Everyone seems so happy today."

"I can answer that." I spun around to see Theo right next to me.

"I don't mean to eavesdrop," he smiled. "That was rude of me, wasn't it? I was just going to say that the actual town coming together didn't happen that long ago. Juniper was the one who incorporated all the little outposts into one community about ten years ago when she arrived. It's taken about that long to get everyone to open up and trust each other. They were used to doing it all alone for a long time."

"I see." Brayson and I continued down the street.

Theo stayed right beside us. "If you don't mind me asking, I've been dying to know where you are from and what your city is like. I've lived here all my life and always dreamed of moving to a city one day."

Brayson excused himself and disappeared into the crowd, leaving me alone to deal with the questions. *Thanks a lot there, friend.*

"Honestly." I looked over the faces of the people milling about the market. "This is much better than the city."

"You only say that because you chose to leave it. It can't be as backwards as this place."

A girl ran by me with ribbons tied in her hair trailing behind her in the wind. "It is though." I looked at Theo earnestly, willing him to understand. "There is no life in the city. No laughter. The streets are filled with forgotten trash. Nothing grows through the abandoned ruins of concrete."

Theo's jaw clenched, reminding me vaguely of Fergus. I unconsciously took a step back and he looked concerned.

"I didn't mean to offend you. It's just so frustrating. The people here don't aspire to be anything more than they are. Everything is stuck in the present, and I know there must be a better future. We have to work toward something bigger." He smiled and gave me a half-hearted shrug. "I'm probably rambling. I apologize. Also, I never introduced myself. My name is Theo."

"Fawn," I said, shaking his outstretched hand. "And don't worry about it. I think out loud too. We already know the future though, it's the here and now that counts."

Theo studied my face. "Are you talking about the realm? That's the future after this one. It's not the future of our lives right now, but I'd be lying if I said I didn't enjoy it there."

My heart skipped a beat, but I made my voice sound as disinterested as possible. I picked up a trinket from a stall and ran my fingers over it. "Oh. The realm. Do you go there often? Is there even a portal here?"

"In this backwoods village?" Theo smirked. "No, but I know a place less than an hour away that has one. I can take you there sometime if you'd like."

"That'd be nice." I set down the beaded necklace and smiled at the shopkeeper. "Some other time maybe. I need to go find my friend." I slipped away through the crowd of market goers leaving Theo standing there staring after me.

*

The haunting melody started once I closed my eyes.

"Vorie," I groaned half awake. "Go see Brayson. He needs you."

"I can't do that yet," she spoke into my ear. I thrashed my arm out at her ghostly essence to make her go away. She started singing again until I sat up and turned on the lamp.

"I'm physically exhausted," I yawned. "Why don't you ever come when I'm awake?"

"It's easier for me this way. When you're asleep you are closer to the realm and I can draw myself to you."

"Well Brayson is probably dead asleep in the other room. Why don't you draw yourself over there?"

"I can't." Vorie frowned. "He won't let me go a second time. He needs space to grieve and heal."

"He probably doesn't see it that way." I crossed my arms. She began to fade. "Stop! Come back. I'm awake now. I'm sure you are right with your new all seeing, all knowing capabilities."

"I can't see everything." She climbed onto the bed and sat beside me. "I'm learning more all the time, but I can't see it all."

"You saw us coming to this place, right?" I smiled at her. "You're doing great by my standards."

Her brow furrowed as she stared out the window. "I think this is what I saw, but I'm not sure. Fergus found me today."

"He what?" I gasped.

"Nothing bad. I mean I still don't trust him, but he just wanted to let me know they were looking for you."

"Who is?" I pulled the blanket up higher around my waist.

"Everyone." Vorie's eyes suddenly glossed over as she turned to the door. "I have to go now."

"Don't!" I cried out as she disappeared. *Great, now I'm never going back to sleep.*

There was a loud knock that caused me to jump off the bed. I scrambled to the door quietly and peeked out the eyehole. Brayson was standing in the hall. My heart returned to its normal pace as I undid the chain latch.

"Mind if I sleep on the couch tonight?" he asked. "I don't want to be alone."

I pulled the top blanket off my bed and tucked him in on the sofa. He fell fast asleep instantly. Not me. I tossed and turned most of the night dreaming I was being chased by wolves.

Chapter 6

∞

The next few weeks passed quickly in a blur of work. There wasn't much time to think as it seemed I was always moving. I learned that in the spring we plant most of the crops and harvest the winter vegetables as they ripen. Fallon used greenhouses and his hundred-acre farm to rotate through the different growing seasons. We plowed fields and weeded the rows. There were animals on the farm too. I shoveled hay and cleaned the coops.

As the days grew warmer, the work became more methodic. My skin darkened under the sun. I never realized how pale I'd always been. The muscles in my tawny arms grew stronger. I felt more powerful and more alive every day.

On Saturdays we worked at the market. Theo began to come talk with me after my shift at the stall. I only saw him on market days because he spent the week driving goods between the towns. The small villages spread throughout the Northwest traded with each other using travelers.

"I've been trying to get Juniper to make a more centralized market like this one so all the villages could come together." Theo leaned back against the wooden bench and crossed one leg over the other.

It was a seriously hot day. My tank top clung tightly to my back and I pulled my hair into a ponytail to get it off my neck as he spoke. He'd talk for hours about his grand ideas to make something big out of this go-nowhere village. Mostly, I just nodded my head. I didn't agree with a lot of his plans, but he was a nice enough guy and it seemed he needed someone to talk to. He didn't fit in with anyone there.

"Even after everyone left for the realm, they still realized we needed places to congregate. And the money the mafia makes from it…" Theo paused to whistle. "They sure knew how to take advantage of that market."

"But look at the problems it comes with." I shifted my legs up off the warm bench. "Just being together isn't enough. People always want more. They need more vices, more control, more competition. People suffer because of it."

"We could do better." Theo smiled fondly at me and I shook my head. He always seemed so childlike in these moments.

"Fawn!" Juniper stood waving me over from across the street. I excused myself from our conversation, leaving Theo alone on the bench.

"You've been spending a lot of time with him lately." She looked at me from the corner of her eye.

"It's not like that." We walked together under the shadows of the abandoned diner's overhanging roof. "I just feel sorry for him. He seems so out of place here."

"Don't feel sorry for him," Juniper scoffed. "He's had an easy life. Too easy probably. He doesn't think anything bad will ever touch him."

We stepped behind Fallon's stall. Brayson stood up after placing a crate of onions under the table. His t-shirt stretched thin across his biceps. His hair had grown longer and was hanging into his eyes. The sun had kissed his face and hardened it, making him seem much older, but laughter lit up his eyes a little more each day. He reached out a calloused hand to shake Juniper's hand.

"You two are doing well," she nodded. "I was a little nervous at first to see how you'd do, but I had a feeling it'd turn out alright."

"Hey Fallon." Juniper caught him in a rare moment of silence as he drifted from one customer to the next. "Do you mind if I steal these two tomorrow? I think it's time they learned some more skills."

Fallon put on a dramatic business face as he pretended to weigh his options. "I suppose," he finally said while winking at me. His wink was awful too and I giggled. "We'll be slowing down for the next month or so anyway. Might as well teach them now before the real work starts with the end of summer harvest."

Brayson and I locked eyes. *Real work?*

*

The open desert stretched before us as we drove further away from the base of the mountain where the sleepy village sat. We kept the windows shut due to the trail of dust the ATVs and Juniper's dirt bike kicked up.

They stopped at the edge of a small ravine. Juniper taught us to shoot one of the M16s and the 30.06 before moving onto the smaller pistols. I preferred the 9mm because it had less of a kick, but I still wasn't very good. Once Brayson figured out the scope, he wasn't half bad. A real smile brightened his face as the men clapped him on the back.

After the guys had their fun teasing me and firing off a few more rounds, they loaded their ATVs up to head home. Juniper told us to hang back as they left.

"Well, it's been almost two months, and no one has come looking for you." She stood with her arms crossed as Brayson and I sat on the tailgate of the truck. "I've been asking around, but there doesn't seem to be much interest in two runaway orphans. That tells me you're either really lucky or not important enough to care about."

"We told you they don't own us anymore," Brayson said as he studied the mountains on the horizon.

"I wasn't born yesterday. You wouldn't have cut out your trackers if you weren't on the run," Juniper sighed. "Fawn sucks at shooting. I'll need her to get better at that to defend this place if trouble ever comes looking for you. I also wanted to get you both out of the hotel, but Mrs. Shaw said she wouldn't hear another word about it." I stared hard at her, wondering where all this was coming from.

"The town held a vote last night and decided to keep you both here if you want to stay for good."

My breath caught in my throat. "They voted to keep us here. Like, they want us to live here?"

Juniper nodded. "You've proved your worth. Just let me know what you plan to do so I can see about making arrangements if you'd like to leave the hotel." She turned toward her bike. "And when you're ready, you can tell me why you really ran. I'm pretty curious about that."

"Can we have some time to give you an answer?" I called out to her as she kickstarted the engine. She nodded once more before peeling out down the dirt road.

"What's there to think about?" Brayson asked as he slid behind the steering wheel. "I want to stay here, and I honestly think they need us to stay."

"I think we are getting off too easy." I chewed the hangnail from my finger. "They aren't just going to let me go for what I did. I don't want the people in the town to get hurt because of me."

The landscape zoomed past the window and I sent out a silent wish that Vorie would come talk to me soon. I hadn't seen her since the night Brayson came back to sleep on the couch. *Hopefully she didn't get the wrong idea. On second thought, she knows me better than that.*

"We don't even know that anyone is chasing you." Brayson turned the truck onto the main road. "Juniper said she was looking into it. I trust her judgement."

"I do too." Tears of frustration welled in my eyes. I couldn't tell Brayson about what Vorie had said. He was just starting to smile again and seemed happy here. I didn't want to bring that all crashing down on him. I stared silently out the window until we reached the hotel.

*

"You're staying, right?" Oleen grabbed my arm and spun herself around as soon as we walked into the kitchen.

"Sit down girl." Mrs. Shaw smacked at her with the tea cloth. "Give them a minute to breathe. Of course they are staying."

"I want to stay," Brayson said. I could feel his eyes boring a hole into the back of my head.

"Me too." I smiled tightly. "But if we do, we should think about moving somewhere more permanent."

"Nonsense." Mrs. Shaw put her hands on her hips. "I wouldn't have any of that talk at the meeting and I won't have it here now. This is your home if you want it. We can use the extra help and your rooms would just sit empty waiting for you to come back if you ever left us." Mr. Shaw flung open the back door as we took our seats at the table.

"Thank you," Brayson said as he took the plate of cornbread from Mrs. Shaw. "We still have some things to discuss before we make our final decision."

"What's there to discuss?" Mr. Shaw sat at the head of the table while grinning at his wife. "The decision has already been made. You're staying here with us. Don't argue with Mrs. Shaw or she'll stop feeding you."

I watched their laughter and smiling faces all through dinner with a lead weight on my heart.

*

"We need to give them an answer at some point." Brayson leaned against the wooden fence looking down into the goat pen.

I sat in the dirt bottle feeding the kids. Their tiny hoofs dug into my outstretched legs as they tumbled over each other trying to get more to drink. Brayson spent the past week learning to hunt with Akon while I chose to stay on the farm. I lifted the kid by his full squishy belly and placed him at my feet.

"Juniper asked me again this morning what our plans are." Brayson draped his arms over the fence and sighed. "I don't understand why you are so hesitant to say yes."

"I'm worried." I picked up the final goat to feed. He latched onto the rubber nipple while I stroked the gray streak of fur on his head. "What if they get hurt because of us?"

"You're overthinking this, Fawn. Juniper isn't stupid. She knows this could be a risk, but she asked us to stay anyway. I honestly don't think the mafia can even find us. It's a big world and without our trackers we pretty much just vanished," Brayson chuckled softly. "And do you think those thugs would travel all the way out here?"

I shook my head smiling at the thought of the dust on their leather shoes. "You really want to stay, don't you?" He gave me a hopeful smile.

"Fine," I whispered while closing my eyes. "Let's stay."

*

Theo stood at the market stall entrance holding a long-stemmed orange poppy in his hand.

"What's with the flower?" Fallon walked over and blocked my view of it. "You think she's got any use for a flower? Come back with something worthwhile and maybe I'll let her leave." I laughed as I pushed my way past him. Theo's cheeks were red.

"Don't be rude," I scolded the old man playfully. "Who says the flower is even for me?"

Theo extended his arm out and handed it to me. "Of course it's for you." He cast a worried glance back at Fallon as we walked down the street. "Who else would it be for?"

I inhaled the scent of the sweet blossom and then tucked it behind my ear. "Thank you. It's lovely. Fallon is right though. I don't need any flowers."

Theo kept his eyes on the pavement under our feet. "It's not about needing them. I wanted to do something nice for you. I was also wondering if you wanted to have a drink with me tonight. There is this nice club I found in the realm. I can pick you up at…"

I didn't hear the rest of his words. A low hum filled my ears and my heart thudded hard against my ribcage. The people laughing and shopping on the crowded street blurred into unrecognizable shapes.

Walking down the center of the road was a man dressed in all black. The summer sun illuminated his outline giving him a mirage type glow. His piercing green eyes lit up and a playful smile came to his lips as he spotted me.

My breathing felt shallow and fear mixed with excitement kept me frozen to the spot. From somewhere deep inside I heard the command to run, but I couldn't make my feet move. Theo must have noticed because he put his hand on my shoulder and shook me gently.

"Are you alright?" His words were distant, under water, even though he was right next to me. "We can move to the shade if you're hot."

I stood without blinking as I watched him take each determined step to close the distance between us.

"There you are little deer." His voice teasingly caressed my skin.

"Alister." His name came out of my lips as a desperate whisper.

Chapter 7

∞

"What are you doing here?"

"What do you think?" Alister's eyes never left mine. I felt Theo tense beside me.

"Do you know this man?" Theo asked.

Alister raised an eyebrow as he stared at me intently. "Another one?" he smirked.

I felt the heat rise in my cheeks and folded my arms across my chest. "That's none of your business." His lip curled into a teasing smile as we stood toe to toe on the street.

"Is there a problem, Fawn?" Theo placed his hand on the small of my back. The touch jarred me, and I stepped to the side away from his reach. Alister's smile grew bigger and he broke our stare to take an uninterested glance at Theo.

"No problem." I smiled sweetly, hoping to stop a real problem from starting. "Alister is an old friend. I just didn't expect to see him here. Will you excuse us? We have some catching up to do." Theo gave a final look to Alister before bowing back into the passing crowd.

"What do you want?" I glared at him after Theo was gone.

"You," he whispered.

"How did you even find me?"

"Can we go somewhere to talk?" he sighed as he reluctantly turned his attention to the market goers surrounding us. "Somewhere we won't be overheard."

I nodded and led him off the main street. Before we passed the last brick building, I caught a glimpse of Juniper watching us leave. *Crap*.

We walked to the outskirts of the little village and came to a small hill overlooking the open field. The bugs danced and hummed around the sagebrush. I sat down on the dirt, keeping a good distance between Alister's body and mine. Every passing second that he was here made me want to reach over and touch him, but I had to keep my wits about me until I got my answers.

"You look beautiful, little deer." He reached toward the flower in my hair and paused before trailing his hand down the air next to my face. He might as well have caressed my skin with the current I felt during the motion. "You seem so much more alive if that's even possible."

I ignored his comment and focused instead on the rocks near my hand. "How did you find me?"

"Vorie told me." He placed his arms on top of his knees.

"I doubt that," I huffed. "How would you even find her? She wouldn't go to any of the communal spots."

"Actually, she did." Alister looked out over the open field. "She wanted help with her skills and visited a spirits only joint I recommended, but that's not how I found her. I tried to explain this before, but you never paid attention. There are some things you don't understand. Bad things, and maybe some good things, about this world and the realm."

"I'm sorry I was too busy serving serial killers drinks and burying my best friend to care about your elitist lifestyle." I rolled my eyes. "Did you come all this way to talk to me about your party tricks again?"

"No. I came all the way here to tell you that you aren't safe and that you need to come with me."

"That's not going to happen," I laughed.

"Listen to me. This is bigger than me wanting you. There are forces here you can't begin to understand without some training." His tone was harsh. "Remember the symbols on the grates at The Nocere? That was just a small taste of what could happen with the portal technology. There is so much more to this world. Think conjurors and magic spells. I was able to get in touch with Vorie using a simple summoning spell. Think of how easy it would be for them to do the same thing to find her."

I clasped my hand over my mouth. "Is she okay?"

"She's fine. I gave her this rudimentary protection spell. It should hold for a while, but she needs to stay low until I can figure out a way to clear your name and get you out of this mess."

"Are you some kind of witch?" I stared at him wide-eyed.

"Of course not." He narrowed his eyes. "I just know how to read."

"Yeah, I didn't think you were," I smiled. "That's a little farfetched. Anyway, it'll probably be impossible to clear my name considering I actually did blow up the club."

"I know you did," Alister chuckled. "You were the only thing in there strong enough to pull something like that off. Unfortunately, that place had both mafia and government ties, so you have both sides of the coin against you." He leaned back on his elbows and winked. "Luckily for you, I know someone who works in the government."

"I can't just leave." I shook my head. "I told them I would stay. And what about Brayson? What is he supposed to do?"

"I took care of that for you," Alister shrugged. "I got the blueprints back to the office.

They think the death of his fiancé was too much for him and he left town."

"I'm sure they'll be able to connect the dots when they figure out who Vorie is to me. We all grew up in the same orphanage, remember?'

Alister studied the desert before us silently. "I'll figure something out," he finally said.

"You don't have to." I stood up and brushed away the tiny pebbles embedded in my hands. "I've already made up my mind. This is my home now and I'll never go back to the realm until my life is truly over. Come with me." I turned and started walking back to town. "There are some people I want you to meet."

*

Mrs. Shaw was moving about the kitchen. Her gray hair was plastered to her wrinkled face from the warmth of the stove coupled with the heat of the day.

"I brought a friend for dinner if you don't mind," I said as I pulled Alister into the room.

Mrs. Shaw looked him over distrustfully. "Carry the slop bucket out back to the bin and bring in some more wood for the stove. Then maybe I'll think about feeding you." She lifted the handle on the waste pail and swung it toward him. Alister grimaced as he caught it and I burst into laughter.

"The bin is just outside in the alley," I giggled. "You're lucky she didn't make you wash the windows." He mumbled something under his breath as he walked out the back door.

"He's too skinny," Mrs. Shaw remarked as the screen door closed behind him. "Why don't you get yourself one of them nice boys who work in the field? Or maybe a hunter. Someone who knows how to provide." She stirred the pot on the stove.

"He's just passing through," I reassured her as I began to shuck the corn. "Nothing more than a visitor from my old life." She pressed her lips tightly together as she continued to cook.

Mr. Shaw and Brayson came home from the market just as Alister entered the door with his arms full of wood. Brayson's eyes widened as he looked from Alister's face to mine.

"Don't worry," I smiled. "He just came to tell us that Vorie is doing well." I stared at him intently, hoping he'd wait to ask questions. He nodded.

We set the table quickly as Mrs. Shaw began to bring the food over. Oleen came bouncing into the kitchen and froze awkwardly upon seeing Alister there.

"Close your mouth girl," Mrs. Shaw said. "You'll catch a fly."

Oleen clamped her jaw shut and took her seat at the table. She couldn't take her girlish gaze off Alister and coyly touched his hand as he handed over the dinner rolls. He dropped his eyes to his plate in embarrassment. Brayson and I laughed softly at his misfortune.

"You said Vorie is well," Mr. Shaw spoke after chewing a mouthful of corn. "Why hasn't she come to visit our boy then?"

Alister looked at me in confusion and I bumped my knee into his leg to keep him quiet, instantly regretting the jolt of electricity that ran up my thigh. I could tell he felt it too by the steadying breath he took.

"I ran into her by accident," Alister said. "She hasn't wanted to make the journey back here until she feels it would be easier for her to leave again."

Brayson pushed the food around on his plate. "I figured as much. How did she look?"

"Beautiful," Alister said softly.

"She always does," Brayson nodded.

"Do you frequent the realm often?" Mr. Shaw asked, watching Alister with an eagle eye.

"Unfortunately, yes. My job requires me to travel there. Recent events have made my visits more frequent than I'd like," Alister sighed.

"What is it you do for work, son?" Mr. Shaw continued to probe.

"I'm in training for congress."

"The government," Mrs. Shaw sneered. "That's not real work."

Alister looked humbly at the food on the table. "You seem to be doing well. Do you not require government assistance in any form?"

Mr. Shaw chuckled. "Don't need any assistance from any government. Never have, never will."

"Fascinating." Alister set his fork gently on the napkin. "And you have no portals in this town, so I assume you don't travel to the realm. Does the mafia not help you either?"

"Mafia. Government. They are both the same," Mr. Shaw smirked. "No use for either of them. We've always been self-sufficient."

"What do you do in congress?" Oleen interrupted to ask. Her voice was an octave higher than normal and she bat her eyelashes at him while she spoke.

"Not much now. I mostly run errands. Someday I hope to represent the people fairly by creating programs and changing laws to better suit their needs."

"Well you can leave us alone if you don't mind," Mrs. Shaw gave Oleen a scolding look. "The government may work well for those east coast areas, but over here we like things the way they are."

I stared fascinated at the conversation. It seemed there was a whole other side to the world that I knew nothing about. We'd been told there were still governments. These small ruling bodies around the world, but who they ruled was beyond me. The mafia controlled our neighborhood and that's all I've ever known.

"At the risk of sounding naive?" I looked nervously to Alister's face. "What exactly does the government do?"

"Nothing here," Mr. Shaw said. "They'll send a representative out every so often to offer us assistance in exchange for making them our leaders. We tell them where they can shove that every time they come."

Alister smiled. "There are people, businesses, and towns that thrive under our regulations and assistance. The mafia has run rampant for far too long and some of us are working toward bringing an end to that chaos."

"The mafia and government have been in bed with one another for so long they…"

"Husband. Mind your tongue," Mrs. Shaw warned.

"He's right though," Alister said sadly. "There are some weeds we need to pull, which is why I'm so dedicated to what I am trying to do."

*

Oleen and I helped to clear the dishes while Mr. Shaw napped in his chair. Alister and Brayson stepped outside to stack wood.

"Why are there no portals in this town?" I asked as I dried a plate.

"There was one." Mrs. Shaw's weathered hands fished in the soapy bucket for the silverware. "When I was a little girl there was a portal at the gas station. My father and some other townsmen tore it down when the power grid went offline. It seemed like everyone was already gone by that time. Dad said it started out slowly, but when places began to shut down and people stopped working, the rest decided to go too."

"Do you remember the way the world was before?"

Mrs. Shaw shook her head. "It's always been this way for as long as I can remember, but my father told me stories. I'll tell them to you sometime." She dried her hand on her apron and walked over to dig out a room key. "Make sure he leaves in the morning." She reluctantly placed the cool metal in the palm of my hand. "He doesn't belong here."

"I know," I smiled as I held her hand. "You are always right."

*

Alister and I sat talking in my room as the night settled heavy on the village around us. He was full of questions wondering how the town was so self-sufficient. I told him about the town meeting and their voting session, but since we'd only been to one, I couldn't offer any more information than that. It all was so fascinating to him.

Brayson wanted to know every detail about Vorie and made Alister promise to tell her he loved her.

"Do you really think they won't come after us?" Brayson stood yawning with his hand on the doorknob.

"I think you are safe here," Alister reassured him.

"Why'd you lie?" I quietly asked Alister after Brayson left the room.

"I didn't." He stretched out comfortably on the couch. His eyes followed me as I walked over to the window. "I think he is safe here. I don't think you are. There's been talk about the girl who blew up The Nocere. Some high-ranking mafia member was there that night and he's got a vendetta to settle." The image of the monster's cruel smile flashed across my mind.

I shook my head. "I'll fight them if they come. We'll all fight them. Juniper said we would."

"You'd really put this whole town in jeopardy?" There was no malice in his voice, but I felt the question stab me.

"They said it was okay," I whispered as I looked down at the street below. The desert wind blew a strong gust against the glass. Rage at the past few months, at the life I'd been forced to live, slowly built up inside of me.

"And I'll learn to shoot. I'll protect myself." I spun around to face him.

"I have no doubt about that little deer," Alister smiled. "But I can teach you something better than shooting. Come with me. You'll have the best instructors. You can learn to harness your powers in the realm. The world is going to need you with the way everything is going."

"You keep saying this like I care about the realm. I've seen the realm and I have no desire to ever go back. And all your talk about witches and magic, these are just fairy tales. More illusions in the realm."

A dark cloud passed over his face. "I've seen what they can do with it. This is no fairy tale."

"Well I don't see how these cheap party tricks are going to help," I shrugged. "I live in the real world now. It's what I've wanted all my life and I'm not ready to give it up. One day we will all have to live in the realm. I'll practice what you want me too then."

"By then it might be too late. And what about me?" He raised his eyes up to meet mine and bit his bottom lip, causing my toes to curl against the rug. "Don't you want to come with me?" The words danced over my skin and coiled in the pit of my stomach.

"No," I said weakly. "I can't right now."

A growl came from deep in his throat as he stood up from the couch. "Then I'll leave you now, little deer." He took a small box from his pocket and placed it on the table. "If you need me let me know."

I looked in awe at the little black box. I knew what it was, but I'd never used one before. I guess I never had anyone to call.

"Alister, I…" The words left my lips before I could stop them. He crossed the room in two long steps.

Placing his thumb under my chin, he tilted my face up toward his. The wave of sensation ran down my neck and into my spine causing my knees to buckle. He placed his free arm around my waist, pulling our bodies closer together and keeping me upright.

"I want you to come with me," he whispered the words against my lips.

"Did you ever figure out why it feels like this?" I asked breathlessly.

"I did." His bottom lip gently teased my mouth open. "Except, I won't tell you why until you agree to be mine."

"Wait. Be yours?" I pried myself from his embrace despite my own body screaming out against me. I could feel the tension of his restraint as he let me go. "I belong to no one."

He groaned painfully as he quickly leaned over to kiss my forehead. Then he walked out the door, leaving me to stand there shaking with the impression of his lips still burning on my skin.

Chapter 8

∞

Alister's room was empty in the morning.

"He's so handsome," Oleen reminisced at the breakfast table. "I hate that he had to go."

I let the oatmeal drip from my spoon back into the bowl, thinking about the phone he'd left in my room. *Would it be crazy to try and use it right now?* There was so much more I wanted to talk to him about. *Did he find Roger in the realm? Did he know the Marley Macavay guy who killed him? Why do I miss him so much already?*

"It was for the best," Mrs. Shaw concluded. Oleen's freckled forlorn face with her pouting lip mirrored the emptiness my heart felt about the situation too.

*

Brayson and I placed the empty barrels in the back of his truck. Most of the villagers were on a well system and paid us in water for the odd jobs we'd done around their homes. Mrs. Shaw said they used to barter her homemade candles and bread for the water before we arrived. I knew most of the families made their own candles, so I didn't press for the details of the previous transactions. The Shaws would hate to know they were given any sympathy.

We tied down the last barrel and Brayson ran inside to grab the bag of goods that Mrs. Shaw prepared for Emily's aging mother. I stood leaning against the side of the truck, daydreaming about what would have happened had Alister stayed the night.

"I'm not good enough for you, is that it?"

I looked up from my daze to see Theo stumbling across the street. "Excuse me?"

"You're not excused," Theo slurred. "I saw him in your room last night through the window. You've been leading me on for weeks. Pretending you're some stupid farm girl like the rest of the females here. No aspirations, no desire to be better than this shithole town. But you let some city boy with fancy clothes into your bedroom."

I put my hands up to stop his body from crashing into me. The smell of liquor hot on his breath clouded around my face.

"I think you have the wrong idea," I said as I held him steadily on his feet. "But I never led you anywhere. I told you I wasn't interested in being more than friends."

Heads began to peek out from the other windows and doors to see what all the commotion was. I used one hand to wave them away as I looked sternly into Theo's eyes.

"You're drunk right now. Why don't you go sleep this off and we will talk later?" I glanced over to the hotel. Brayson stepped out from the entrance followed by Mr. Shaw with his rifle in hand. "It's alright guys. I've got this." I smiled at them reassuringly. Theo wobbled backwards and I held him up by the shoulder.

"Don't touch me you dumb bitch," Theo yelled. Hot saliva splattered my face. Brayson rushed forward and wrapped his arm around Theo's neck as he dragged him away. I wiped the alcohol tainted spit from my cheeks.

"Yeah, that's right," Theo laughed. "You're just a stupid little orphan bitch."

Red anger seared my vision as I rushed toward him. Someone caught me from behind, pinning me by my arms. I struggled hard against the hold.

"Let me go," I screamed.

"Walk it off," Juniper whispered in my ear. "Let it go. Let's go take a walk."

I hadn't seen her come up behind me. I instantly felt embarrassed and stopped fighting. She held me by my shoulder until we walked down the side street and then she relaxed her grip.

"You alright?" Juniper asked as we slowed down our pace.

"I'm fine. I didn't mean to snap like that." My head hung low as I spoke.

"He was out of line," Juniper said. "But maybe next time you should stay in control of that temper."

"Yeah, I need to work on that." I put my hands in my pockets as we walked. "I can't believe he called me an orphan bitch. I swear I never did anything to let him think I was interested in him that way."

"You're a pretty girl," Juniper sighed. "I'm sure it won't be the last time someone gets the wrong idea. Speaking of intentions…" She stopped walking at the end of the street. "Do I need to worry about the dark and mysterious stranger who showed up yesterday?"

"He's just an old friend." I shook my head. "He won't be coming around anymore."

"Hmph," she smirked. "With the way he looked at you like a cougar closing in on a kill, I'm surprised he'd give up that easy." I looked up at her slowly and the pain must have been written on my face.

"I'm sorry," she said softly. "You want him too."

"It doesn't matter now." I turned and began to head back toward the town center. "Maybe in another life it would have worked, but not in this one."

We walked back onto Main Street. Everyone was going about their morning business as if nothing ever happened. Brayson sat waiting in the cab of the truck.

"Hey Juniper," I called out as she walked away. "Can I come shooting with you sometime again?"

"Sure," she laughed. "Just as long as you promise not to shoot Theo."

*

The late summer sun beat down on my shoulders as we worked to harvest the fields. My hands were calloused beneath my work gloves, but the extra padding helped as I dug the rows of potatoes up. We yanked the roots free from the loosened soil and tossed them into the wheelbarrows to carry back to the barn.

The squash patches and sweet corn fields were also ready to harvest. We spent weeks picking the remaining vegetables and preparing the back field for the onions we'd sow over the winter. The vine ripened tomatoes came away full and juicy in our hands. More people from the town gathered at Fallon's and Mazier's farms to help. Songs and laughter filled the fields as we struggled under the burden of feeding us all.

My back ached every time I woke up and Brayson barely spoke more than a grunt as we drove to the farm before sunrise each morning. It was hard, there is no other word for it, but I realized I didn't have the time or energy to think. For that, I was grateful.

One day, the work began to dwindle. Fallon cooked a giant hog on a spit over an open fire. We had a celebration that night, feasting on smoked meat and grilled corn dipped in butter. Mazier's wife brought over a barrel of her famous mead. We drank and danced around the fire until late in the night.

I sat on the ground sipping the overly sweet mead. Through the flames, I watched as Brayson twirled Oleen around in a silly little dance. I don't think I'd ever seen him dance before. My heart was happy, and I sent up my usual silent hope that Vorie was watching. My body ached and my hands were scarred, but my stomach was full, and I was at peace.

*

"Get down." Juniper placed her hand on my head, causing me to drop the crate of produce I was holding back onto the tailgate of the truck.

"What?" My smile fell as I turned to her in confusion.

"I said get down." Her voice was sharp. I quickly did as I was told.

The market was alive that day, fuller than I'd ever seen it. The neighboring towns had gotten wind of our weekly event and they came to participate. The few stalls we normally had were surrounded by various vendors. Farmers competing with their late summer harvest, weavers, candlemakers, blacksmiths- the street was filled with new faces. I'd hear talk of shutting it down and returning to the way it once was, but everyone was so happy bartering their homemade wares that I didn't see the problem.

"Why am I hiding behind the truck?" I whispered to Juniper. I tried to peer around the side to see what was bothering her.

She grabbed me by the chin. "Do you want to get caught?"

"Caught by who?"

Brayson came rushing toward us in a crouched position from behind the back of the produce tables. "Fallon is talking to them now," he whispered to Juniper. "We have some time."

"Talking to who?" I asked in frustration.

He finally turned and spoke quietly in my ear. "There's two guys from the mafia. I heard them say they were just checking the market out, but they have a picture of someone they are hoping to find."

"Shit." I placed my hand on the truck to keep from falling over. "What do we do?"

Juniper leaned calmly against the vehicle as if she hadn't a care in the world. "They are distracted right now," she said without moving her lips. "Get to the edge of town and wait for me in the field. I'll come find you two when they leave."

"What if they don't leave?" My eyes jumped from Brayson's face to Juniper's back. "What if someone tells them we are here?"

"Don't you trust the people you live with?" She reached over to grab the crate I'd left discarded. "No one will give you away. Now go. Fast. Stay low." She hoisted the crate onto her hip and slowly walked toward Fallon's stall.

Two men wearing gray slacks and mirrored sunglasses with gold chains hanging against their crisp white shirts stood holding a paper in front of Fallon's face.

"Never seen her before in my life." Fallon's voice boomed above the noise of the crowd. The men turned to Juniper who sashayed in front of them while carrying the box of tomatoes. She giggled as they questioned her. *I didn't even know she could giggle.*

"Now's our chance." Brayson tugged at my arm. We crouched as we rushed past the last of the market stalls. Then we ran so fast my lungs started burning as we raced to the boulders at the back of the empty field.

Dusk began to fall and still we sat there waiting.

"We should have stayed up there," I said as I traced the outline of the mountain ridge with my eyes. "We never should have come here. What if they get hurt?"

Brayson had been silent for most of the wait. I knew I needed to stop speaking my fears out loud. He'd been through more than enough already and I didn't want to add to his stress. It's just my mouth goes a mile a minute when I'm anxious.

"No one is getting hurt." Juniper's soft voice made us jump. "You two are going to stay with me tonight though. The thugs got a room at the hotel." My heart dropped to my stomach as I thought of Mrs. Shaw having to deal with those men.

"Don't worry." Juniper read my thoughts. "They'll be fine, but I'm not sure those mafia guys will ever want to experience that kind of hospitality again."

*

We waited until the dark was firmly set before leaving the safety of the rock formation. Using the light from the moon, we crept back into town. Juniper's house was a small one room cottage. She lit some candles and then opened a few jars of homemade venison chili which she heated over the wood stove.

"Thanks for feeding us," I said gratefully.

The cottage was sparsely furnished, but rows of canvases lined the walls along the edges of the floor. At first, I thought she collected art, but then I noticed each acrylic scene carried colors and themes that matched the surrounding ones.

"Did you make all these?" I asked while holding one of the decaying tree series in my hand. Juniper tossed a sleeping bag and some blankets from the hallway closet onto the couch.

"Yes." She looked at the piece I was holding fondly. "I like to paint whenever I have the time. It's a useless hobby, but it calms me down."

"These are really good." Brayson studied the building series hung on the back wall. There were towering structures depicting skyscrapers and overpasses. "Where are you from?"

Juniper smiled. "Why don't you start by telling me your story? Then maybe I'll tell you mine." Brayson gave me a pleading look.

"Are you sure you want to hear it?" I sighed as I sat down at the table. "We'll probably have to leave after you know what happened."

She crossed her arms and leaned against the wall. "Whatever it is can't be that bad, but I do need to know what we're up against."

I put my head into my hands. "We're from the orphanage in LA. The city is mostly empty and the area we lived in was run by the mafia. Sometimes the orphans who graduate out of service stick around, but there are portals everywhere and I think the temptation is too much. Most of them leave to the realm. We do have a lot of Can't Commits and I tried to keep them fed." Juniper arched an eyebrow.

"It's what we call the ones who don't want to live in this world but can't fully commit to living in the realm," Brayson answered.

"I've dealt with a few of those in my day." Her eyes were distant. "People who only come back to keep their bodies alive. The name fits." She nodded for me to continue.

"Vorie and Genie are my best friends. We grew up together in the orphanage. They are my family." I traced the ridges on the wooden table with the pad of my finger. "When I was young, I tried to run away. I cut out my tracker and hid in an alley while they walked right past me. I would have stayed there all night and probably gotten away, but there was a man in the dark alley too. Not a man, a monster."

Brayson's jaw clenched as he walked to the front of the room. He stood there with his back to me. I'd told him what happened on our drive out of the city, but the wound was still just as fresh. Juniper's face was sharp and defensive. Her concern warmed my heart.

"Nothing happened. I bit his hand as he tried to grab me. Then I ran screaming down the streets until I found the mafia. They added an extra year to my sentence. When I turned eighteen, the store didn't want me anymore, so I got this new assignment at The Nocere. Brayson is a genius." I smiled at his back. "He was pulled from the orphanage young because he's a natural architect. He and Vorie were engaged…" I realized I was rambling and tried to bring myself back on track.

"The Nocere was a club in the in between. It was built for killers and people who like hurting others to gather in one place. Under the stage were metal grates with symbols on them which captured murdered spirits as they crossed over to the realm. The spirits couldn't leave. They were trapped there and tormented when they should have been at peace. I was trying to find a way to help and then Vorie was murdered. Her soul got stuck there." I paused to breathe.

"I shouldn't have done it, but when the monster from the alley showed up at the club saying he killed Vorie thinking she was me, I just snapped. I burned the whole thing to the ground. Then we ran. This was honestly our dream all along. We'd been planning to leave once my contract was up. Me,

Vorie, Brayson, and we were trying to convince Genie…" Saying her name brought a lump to my throat. *I really miss Genie.* I swallowed hard and looked over to Juniper. I couldn't read her face.

"Okay," she finally whispered. "Thank you for telling me." She moved over to the table and pulled out the opposite chair. "I thought the in between was a myth."

"I did too, but apparently they were testing it before the whole world fell apart." I pulled my legs up onto the seat and wrapped my arms around them. "There was nothing else there besides the club. Well, I guess there is nothing there at all anymore."

"Are you a destroyer?" she asked.

"No. Fergus is a destroyer. I worked with him at the club. I don't know what I am. I can see through glamour and make stuff explode," I smirked. "Oh, sometimes I can make the air shake."

Juniper's face remained impassive, but I saw the slightest hint of worry crease her brow before it disappeared.

"Alister, the stranger who came to town, wants me to go learn how to use this stuff, but I don't see the point. I'll just figure it out when it's really my time to go to the realm."

"I see. And who is Alister in all of this?"

"He's a government trainee or something." I shrugged. "I met him the first night I worked at the club when he and his aunt came looking for Roger. He was…" My voice trailed off as I remembered Roger's warning to never speak aloud the name of who killed him. "Roger was trapped there too. I like Alister, but it's never going anywhere." Juniper nodded but she could tell I was hiding something.

I looked nervously at my hands. "Alister says Brayson is in the clear. He returned the blueprints that Brayson borrowed."

"I believe that. The men just had a photo of you, but they said it was a possibility you were traveling with a male."

"Should I leave then?"

"Don't be stupid. This is your home. We'll figure out whatever comes." She stood up from the table. "It's late. Why don't we get some sleep?"

"What's your story?" Brayson asked before she walked down the hall.

"Not as interesting as your story," she smiled. "I did my time in the orphanage and tried to save people who didn't want to be saved. Then I came out here to escape it all. These are good people, but they didn't know how to work together. I helped them with that. This is my home now. It's nothing like Seattle and I prefer it that way." The word "Seattle" hung in the air until I slipped into a deep and dreamless sleep.

Chapter 9

∞

Brayson and I waited inside Juniper's house the next morning while she went to check the hotel. The mafia men were gone, but she didn't want to risk us being seen so she drove us out to Fallon's farm for the day. Someone moved Brayson's truck out there and it sat parked behind the barn.

*

"Good riddance," Mrs. Shaw said at the dinner table that night. "Horrible, lazy, rude men. They left the room in shambles and tried to pay with credits for their stay. What in the world do we need those for?"

"But Granny, you still have a tracker." Oleen looked wistfully at the old woman's arm.

"It's there just in case." Mrs. Shaw waved her hand dismissively. "But you don't see me using it now, do you?"

*

Juniper met us out front of the hotel as we were getting ready to leave for work the next morning.

"Brayson, I have a new assignment for you. Mr. Bankole is starting a construction job this week building a new house. He said he needs the help and I thought you may be interested." Brayson's eyes lit up.

"I'm taking Fawn with me today. Head on over to his place. He's expecting you."

I stood awkwardly waiting on the sidewalk as he drove away. It felt like when the director was upset at the orphanage. I was nervously waiting for the punishment to come.

"Get in." Juniper pointed to a Jeep. I'd never seen her drive anything but her dirt bike and wasn't sure if I should be worried.

We drove up the mountain pass in silence. By the time the sun rose, and she pulled off the main road, I was convinced she was going to tell me I needed to leave. She parked the Jeep and turned off the engine.

"If I were in your shoes, I would have destroyed that place too." She pulled her long black hair into a bun on the back of her head. "But the weird powers you have in the realm aren't going to do you any good here. Let's practice on your shooting now and then I'm going to teach you how to fight."

The tension eased from my shoulders, but it was quickly replaced with the fear that she was going to kick my ass.

*

    We hiked through the beaten deer paths carrying two long guns. Juniper showed me how to hunt and how to keep moving or blend into my surroundings so I wouldn't be found. We spent hours sweating as we climbed rocky patches and rested for brief moments in the cool shade of the pine trees.

    She had me aim for targets half unseen. I still missed most of the time, but it was easier without the group of men teasing me. I was starving by midday. Juniper shot a rabbit. Then she showed me how to build the fire and field dress the meat. We charred strips on sticks over the flames. It was a far cry from Mrs. Shaw's cooking, but I appreciated the food.

    In the late afternoon, we made our way back down to the Jeep. Working on the farm had given me a strength I never knew I had, but hiking the rigorous terrain tested my leg muscles in ways I never thought possible. My backside was sore and twitching as I climbed into the passenger seat.

    "You did good today. Not one complaint." Juniper started the engine. "I'm proud of you. We'll come back up here again, but tomorrow I'll come get you and we will work on some hand to hand fighting skills."

    "Thank you," I said, barely mustering the energy to smile. "I know you don't have to help me, and honestly I'm not sure why you bother, but I really appreciate everything you've done."

She stared intently through the windshield as she drove down the mountain. "You remind me a lot of my younger self. If I can prevent someone from having to deal with the things that I did, it's my duty to help."

*

Mary had a little lamb…

"Why?" I groaned loudly into my pillow as the haunting melody drifted through the room. "I've been calling out for you to come visit me for months now, and you pick the one night I need sleep more than I ever have in my life to show up."

Vorie sat at the foot of my bed. "I'm sorry. Things have been complicated lately."

"Why do you sound so sad?" I sat up into the darkness of the room. The aura of Vorie's spirit pulsed weakly against the night. "Alister came to see me. He said he conjured you or something. I didn't know people could do that. But he said you were doing good."

"I'm fine," she smiled. "Don't worry about me. There is so much about this world and the realm we didn't know Fawn. That's why I had to come tonight."

"I wish you'd come more often. Are you going to see Brayson soon? Oh, and I was going to ask you if you've been to see Genie."

"I'll go see him tomorrow night. I promise. Just don't say anything to him. And yes, I've been to see Genie."

"How is she?" My voice peaked with excitement. "Can you tell her I miss her when you see her next time? Maybe she'd like it here in town. You could tell her where we are."

Vorie shook her head sadly. "She's not going to come here. Craton asked her to marry him and she's moving to his family's town in Virginia."

"She's getting married without us?" I gasped.

"She's hurt right now," Vorie said softly. "Give her some time and things will work out."

"Is that one of your all-seeing ghost tricks?" I rolled my eyes. "I'm hurt too. She refused to come with me when I needed her."

"Just give it time," she sighed as she got that distant look in her eyes again. "I have to go soon."

"But you just got here," I whined.

"You know I'm always here with you," she laughed.

"Yeah, but I wish it didn't feel like I was always talking to myself."

"You're fine. No one thinks any less of you for being crazy. Listen, I need you to be ready."

"Why? Is there something else coming? More than the two guys you didn't warn me about yesterday."

"Things are about to change. It's for the best. Just try not to be so stubborn and fight everything." Vorie began to fade.

"You could stop with the ghostly warnings and just come hang out with me some time," I said to the empty room.

*

I had some time before Juniper was supposed to arrive that day for our training session. Brayson left early in the morning to head to the construction site. Mrs. Shaw and I were in the kitchen washing the breakfast dishes when we heard the commotion on the street.

"Can you see what's happening out there?" I asked with my face pressed against the lobby window. Mrs. Shaw cracked open the front door.

"Get down!" Juniper screamed as she ran up behind me and shoved the door closed out of Mrs. Shaw's grasp. The kitchen screen door slammed loudly against the frame. I dropped to my hands and knees. Mr. Shaw came in breathing hard and put a finger over his lips before laboring up the staircase.

"What's happening?" I asked Juniper from my position on the floor.

She took a second to catch her breath and put a hand reassuringly on Mrs. Shaw's back. "We might need to get you out of town for the next few days, Fawn. I'm trying to figure out somewhere safe for you to go."

"Are they back? What's going on?" My thoughts were racing.

"There's more of them. I think we need to leave right now," Juniper said.

"I have a phone and someone who can help. Do I have time to get it from my room?"

She nodded. "Hurry."

I raced up the steps and grabbed the box from the small table.

"We've got you surrounded," I heard Mr. Shaw yell as I came back into the upstairs hall. "There's a trained shooter in every window on this street. Leave now and you won't get hurt." My heart was heavy with worry as I ran down the steps.

"I don't know how to use it." I thrust the phone into Juniper's hand. "He said to call if I ever needed him."

She opened the device and stared blankly at the screen. Mrs. Shaw grabbed it from her hand. The box emitted some beeping sounds as she touched it.

"You kids don't know how to do anything," Mrs. Shaw mumbled as she crouched against the wall. Juniper crawled over to me and we both raised our heads slightly to peak over the window seal. The north side of Main Street had a bunch of vehicles blocking the exit. Mafia thugs with their gold chains and suits stood armed in the street in front of the cars.

"We just want the orphan girl," the man in front called out. "Give her to us and we leave."

"I don't know what you idiots are thinking," another voice called from somewhere down the street. "We've got you outnumbered and outgunned. You need to get your guys out of here." My heartbeat pounded loudly in my ears.

"As soon as we have the girl, we'll go," the mafia boss said calmly.

"There are no orphans here," a second voice yelled. "And even if there were, this isn't your jurisdiction."

"Bring him out." The mafia thug directed one of his men to open the back door of a sedan. I gasped as two of the thugs pulled a bound and gagged Theo from the backseat. He hung his head in shame as they paraded him down the street.

"This informant tells me she is here, and she lives in that hotel." He pointed right toward us. Juniper pushed my head down.

"You listen to me and you listen to me good," Mrs. Shaw yelled into the box. "You promise me you'll take care of her. I'll hunt you down if you don't." Juniper motioned for the phone and Mrs. Shaw reluctantly handed it over. She placed it firmly against my ear.

"Hello? Fawn? Is she okay?" Alister's voice came echoing through the speaker. It made me lightheaded to hear it and I wanted to reach through to touch him.

"I'm fine for now," I finally said.

"Fawn, what's going on?"

"The mafia found me. I'm alright for this moment, but I'm going to need to leave soon."

"Can you meet me at the portal near the theatre in Placeville? I'm going there now."

"Placeville. Theatre. Portal." I said the words out loud in confusion.

"I know where it is," Juniper said. "We can be there in a few hours."

"I can meet you there, but I can't go through the portal. I don't have a tracker."

"Don't worry about that. There's another way," Alister said coldly. "I'll wait for you there, little deer. And if anything happens to you, I promise I will find you." Relief filled me at the sound of his words, followed quickly by the guilt that I was dragging him into my mess too.

The men on the street pushed Theo unceremoniously onto the sidewalk. He sat there with tears and snot streaking down his face.

"We don't know who that man is," a third voice shouted from above. "But you aren't taking a step toward that hotel. You'll frighten old Mrs. Shaw to death."

Mrs. Shaw raced to the kitchen and pulled a 9mm pistol out from under the sink. She carried it into the lobby and checked to see that the magazine was still full.

Suddenly, a white van pulled onto Main Street and blocked the southern exit. Two men in business suits calmly stepped from the vehicle. The mafia men pointed their guns at them.

"She's ours," the boss snarled at the two men.

"She's here? Where is she?"

My head was on a swivel as I looked to the newcomers and back to the thugs on the street.

"What the hell is the government doing here?" Juniper's breath was hot right next to my face.

"Maybe Alister sent them." The hope of that being true was quickly crushed.

"Marcus said you'd come," the mafia boss yelled. "She's still indentured so she's ours. This isn't your problem to solve."

"The federal crimes make her our prisoner." The government man raised his pistol.

"We need to go now." Juniper yanked on my arm. The two of us stayed low as we crawled through the hotel lobby. As we rounded the entrance to the kitchen, I heard the blood curdling scream. Juniper and I both froze. *They had Oleen.*

"Send out the orphan or we shoot the child."

Mrs. Shaw held the pistol steadily in her hand as she moved to unlock the front door. Juniper reached to hold me back, but I slipped through her fingers. I rushed through the lobby and pushed Mrs. Shaw back into the room while running as fast as my feet would carry me into the open street.

One of the thugs held a gun to Oleen's head. She was crying and shaking in his arms.

"I'm so sorry," she gasped between broken sobs. "I was in the alley and didn't see them coming."

"Shut up." The man yanked her head to the side. I raised my palms up. My heart was racing, and my mind was a jumbled mess. I had no clue what I was doing, but I couldn't let them hurt her.

"Shh, shh," I soothed the girl. "It's okay. You didn't do anything wrong. I did something wrong.

This is my fault. Please let her go," I begged the men. "I'm right here. Just let her leave."

The boss nodded to the man and he tossed her onto the sidewalk next to Theo like she was nothing more than a rag doll. I held my breath as I watched her scramble to her feet and make it safely into the hotel.

"You two need to leave," the mafia boss yelled to the government officials behind me.

"We're coming with you." The official holstered his pistol. "We need to report where you are taking her."

"Touch one hair on that girl's head and we will shoot every one of you bastards down," Mr. Shaw shouted from the window above me.

"You shoot us all, more will come," the mafia boss laughed. "There'll be no end to this for your town."

I inhaled deeply upon hearing the man's words, knowing he was right.

"It's okay," I yelled as loudly as I could. *At least my voice didn't crack.* "I'm going with them peacefully." The men lowered their weapons as I took the first tentative step down the worn street toward them.

From behind me, I suddenly heard a jarring *braaap, braaap.* It took a second for my mind to register that it wasn't the sound of guns being fired. The air whooshed from my stomach as Juniper slammed me across her lap on top of the dirt bike. The noise from the guns when they did begin to fire was drowned out by the sound of the engine near my face.

She sped down the side street and then raced through the open field. Her chest was pressed hard against my back to hold me still and I tried to cling to her leg for more support. The bike bounced across the uneven terrain and the wind whipped my hair into a million directions, threatening to yank it off.

After what seemed like a lifetime of pure terror, Juniper finally slowed down the bike. She drove us into a small ravine and dropped the kickstand. I immediately fell to the dirt and pushed my fingers deep into the rocky soil, gasping for breath and clinging to the safety of the ground.

"Come on." Juniper shook her head. "They can't follow us out here with their vehicles, but I want to get you to the portal before they start checking the other towns."

I nodded weakly before climbing onto the seat behind her. After I wrapped my arms around her waist, and buried my face against her back, she gunned the death trap out of the ravine and took us through the desert.

Chapter 10

∞

Placeville was a suburb of houses surrounding an old casino and some other business structures. Cars were left parked in the streets giving the place an eerie half alive, half dead feeling. Juniper parked the bike on a ridge overlooking the valley.

"Where is everyone?" I scanned the buildings but could see no movement.

"They're around here somewhere," she sighed. "This part is the ghost town. The few remaining residents survive on the outskirts. I tried to get them to work together a few years back, but there is too much fighting between the older families. They leave us alone so I can't complain."

Juniper turned to face me. "Are you sure you'll be alright with this stranger of yours?"

"I'm not sure I have another choice," I frowned. "Will you tell Brayson that I'm sorry and I'll come back someday?"

"He'll always have a home here with us." She looked out over the highway leading up to the town center. "It doesn't seem like anyone is coming. Let's get you there before they decide to show up."

I climbed back on the bike and she drove us through the forgotten streets. The theatre was behind a shopping complex. Its roof was partially collapsed, but the entrance was still intact. Metal door frames holding broken glass were propped open on the cement steps.

Alister stood in the middle of the archway waiting. I moistened my wind chapped lips with my tongue as we approached. I'd never seem him that dressed down, but he still looked unbelievably good. He raced down the steps as we dismounted.

"Your hair is a mess," he smiled. "What happened?"

"Well, I was on this bike and didn't have a helmet," I shrugged.

"That's not what I mean."

"Oh, that. I don't even know. The mafia showed up and then there were two government guys. They threatened to shoot Oleen if I didn't give myself up. I walked outside. Juniper showed up like a bat out of hell and whisked me away. Now I'm here." I gave him half a smile. "I don't know what I'm supposed to do next."

"Come with me," he offered. His voice was heavy with unspoken promises. I unconsciously took a step back.

"Where are we even going?" I turned to face Juniper. "Maybe this is a mistake. I should just go live in the mountains alone."

There were tears in her eyes. "I wish I had more time to prepare you, but you're not ready for something like that. I have to get back to town and see what the damage is. Just go. Stay low for a while. We can sort this mess out later." She nudged me forward. I wrapped my arms around her and squeezed tightly.

"You're right. I'm sorry. Thank you for everything you've done." When I pulled away from the embrace, the sun reflecting in her teary black eyes gave me a sudden feeling of déjà vu.

"You do look just like her." My jaw dropped. "And she is from Seattle! How did I not put two and two together?" Juniper's brow creased. "Astrid. You two are almost identical except she's my age. I met her when we worked at The Nocere. I swear you both are related."

The roar of engines rumbling down the highway broke up the surreal encounter. Juniper ran to her bike.

"Get her out of here," she yelled to Alister. "I'll try to lead them the other direction." She sped away down the street leaving the scent of exhaust hanging in the air.

"Which one are we taking?" I looked frantically around at the vehicles parked on the street.

"We have to go through the portal." He held out his hand to me.

"I can't go through the portal. I don't have a tracker. I already told you this," I snapped at him. Some of the vehicles began to chase Juniper, but the remaining few were heading our way.

"Just trust me, little deer," he said impatiently. "You can go through with me."

"That's not possible. I'm still alive. The only way to get through the portal without a tracker is to die, and I'm trying really freaking hard to not do that right now."

"Fawn," Alister growled my name. "Stop fighting everything. Just come with me." His words mixed with Vorie's voice and I finally understood her cryptic message.

"Okay," I whispered as the cars came racing down the street. I reached out to grasp his hand and he pulled me through the theatre entrance. The adrenaline from the moment and the heat from our bodies being so close together caused my heart to bang wildly against my ribcage.

"Whatever you do," Alister turned my face up to his and stared at me with his emerald green eyes. He touched his arm against the panel. The familiar buzzing began as it whirred to life. "Do not let go of me."

I nodded as he wrapped his arm around me. Then I nestled deep against his chest. His heart was beating as fast as mine. I laid my ear against it. Warmth, tension, electricity- they all shot through me as we were sucked through the void. I kept my eyes closed tightly.

This isn't right, I thought. *The portal shouldn't have let me in.* Yet, there I was spinning through the abyss of eternity with Alister's heartbeat mirroring my own.

*

"Where are we?" I blinked as I opened my eyes to the blinding sunlight. I was expecting to be somewhere in the realm but there was a portal behind us. It was a nice one too, painted white and tucked beneath a stone archway. "Can I let go now?"

"I don't want you to," Alister whispered against the top of my head. "But yes, you can let go."

We were standing on smooth stone steps overlooking a grassy field. In the distance were oddly shaped statues and buildings overgrown with ivy. I heard birds squawking over the lull of water lapping against the rocks. The air was unnaturally sticky and heavy against my skin.

"Seriously. Where the hell am I?"

"This is Washington D.C.," he laughed. "It's where I live."

"How did I come through the portal without a tracker and pop out on the other side of the map?"

"There is really so much you don't know, little deer." He reached over to tuck a stray lock of hair behind my ear.

I slapped his hand away. "Then enlighten me."

The corner of his lip raised in a playful smile. "I don't know how much you are ready or willing to hear."

"All of it." I folded my arms across my chest. "You said you would tell me if I came with you."

"That's not what I meant by that statement and you know it. If you chose to come with me, I'd divulge the reason why we are drawn to each other. You said yourself, you had no choice."

"I still made the choice." I sat down on the cool steps of the archway. "I've got nothing but time and I'm not moving until you tell me exactly what is going on."

He sat down softly next to me, careful not to let our bodies touch. "What do you want to know first?"

"Start with how I am able to get through the portal."

"I have a feeling you aren't going to believe me."

"Try me," I said.

"Your soul is connected to mine," he whispered. "That's why we can feel each other in the realm where no one else can feel anything. It's also why the physical reaction is so strong on this plane of existence. Our souls intertwine when we are together. I can take you through the portal because we are a part of each other."

"So, soul mates. That's your answer." I put my head on my knees and groaned.

"You can't deny the way you feel about me," Alister winked.

"Yes, you are handsome and yes I want to sleep with you." I rolled my eyes. "But I don't think I'm ready to be tied to you for all eternity. This sounds like something from a fairy tale."

I watched the hurt roll across his face before it was quickly replaced with a neutral expression. "What's your explanation then?" he calmly asked.

"The magic stuff you were talking about sounds a little more plausible to me." I stared at him trying to read his face. "But you don't even know me well enough to be my one true love."

"It's not about love," he smiled. "It's a deeper connection than that. You will always have the choice on who you want to love. I didn't understand it either until Professor Berlin explained it to me the other day."

"Wait." I raised my hand. "The other day?"

"When I went to ask questions about your abilities and tried to figure out why we could feel each other." Alister gave me a look like I was slow. "I guess it was a few months ago now, but you knew I was going to ask. Don't you remember?"

I could literally feel my blood pressure rising. "You mean to tell me that you risked my life by either dragging me through the portal or abandoning me there in the desert with mafia thugs at my back based on some theoretical information that you just learned the other day?"

"I've missed that temper of yours," he chuckled.

"What temper?" I glared at him.

He ran his thumb over his lips to hide his smile. "If it makes you feel any better, Professor Berlin is the smartest man alive. I trust him completely."

"I don't care who he is. You didn't even know if it would work."

"I did know it would work. There is no other explanation for how I feel about you." Alister stood and held out his hand. "And you should care who he is. We are about to go meet him."

*

His black sedan was left parked on the street across from the portal. Alister expertly drove us under broken bridges overgrown with moss and giant trees arching like canopies over the broken roads. Old stone buildings with giant columns holding up the porch roofs lined the road we came to a stop on. The sticky heat smacked me in the face as soon as I exited the vehicle.

"Tell me again why I have to meet this guy." I hesitated as I stared at the towering arched doorway.

"I know you must be nervous." Alister paused on the steps. "I promise this is for your own good. In your life, you weren't given the opportunity to learn all that you could. Professor Berlin is going to give you that opportunity." He pushed the heavy door open.

"I'm sure I've learned a lot more than you," I mumbled under my breath. "We can't all be rich." Inside the ancient stone building the air was unnaturally cold.

"How did this survive?" I looked up at the twenty-foot ceilings.

"It's been here for a long time and still it stands," Alister said. "Just like humanity."

He grabbed my hand and warmth spread through my fingers. I resisted the urge to pull him back to the car as he dragged me up the stairs. The door to the office was open and Alister stepped inside.

"Here she is," he smiled triumphantly to the man who sat behind the desk.

It was dark in the room and it took a moment for my eyes to adjust. The man at the desk, Professor Berlin I presumed, wore thick spectacles, and was surrounded by heavy volumes of books splayed open across the table. His hair was peppered with grey and his bowtie sat crooked in his shirt. He had a nervous quick energy with shifting eyes which I noticed as he suddenly jumped up and rushed over to us.

"There she is," he said in awe like I was something more than a criminal orphan with farmyard dirt stains on my pants and on the run from the mafia. I nervously stepped closer to Alister.

"Oh, you are a lucky young man," Professor Berlin laughed. "Very lucky indeed. Finding a soulmate this early on in your life and such a pretty one nonetheless." I blushed at his words but remained silent. I honestly didn't know what to say.

"Bring her in. Let's have a look at her," the professor insisted. I felt like one of the prized pigs at

Fallon's farm being ushered to slaughter. Thankfully, Alister pulled out a chair for me so I didn't have to stand there awkwardly wringing my hands.

"Our boy informs me that you have some very special talents," he continued to speak as he leaned against the edge of his desk. The light from the ceiling high windows illuminated the dust particles as they moved about the room. I sat silently watching them dance.

"Fascinating," the professor said softly. I looked up to see him studying me.

"I don't have any special talents." I eyed him curiously. "Not in this world at least. In the realm it seems that I can do some party tricks." Alister moaned as he dropped his head into his hands.

"What?" I asked after his dramatic response had ended. "They are just meaningless tricks." Professor Berlin chuckled as Alister looked to him helplessly. I didn't like being a part of their joke.

"I don't know what I'm doing here." I crossed my arms and leaned back in the chair. "I don't care about the realm or these so-called talents. I just want to live my life my way."

"Dear girl," the professor said. "Life here is temporary. The realm is eternal. You will care about this one day. I can promise you that."

"And when that day comes, I'll deal with it."

"Wouldn't you rather prepare now by studying and practicing how best to live out the rest of your existence?" Professor Berlin looked at me intently.

"I'd rather not waste the precious little time I have left in this world."

"Fawn," Alister reprimanded me. "Professor Berlin has spent his entire life studying the realm. I'm sure he'd not like to hear that it is a waste." I turned to glare at him.

"Psh, psh." The professor waved his hand dismissively in the air. "She's not trying to be disrespectful. Tell me girl, what is it that you truly care for in this world?"

I looked down at the callouses that had formed on my palms. "Life," I whispered. "Living. The earth. Humanity. Salvaging what is left of it all and stopping us from completely disappearing as people rush to this illusional dream."

"Fascinating," Professor Berlin nodded. "What if we do a trade? You let me study you and help you enhance your talents. I'll teach you about the world that was and how we used to be. Maybe that will help you accomplish your grand dreams." I looked over to Alister to see if he was laughing at me. His expression was thoughtful as he listened to the professor's words.

"Is that even possible?" I asked. Hope, like the light brush of a butterfly wing, rose inside my chest. Never had I spoken those words aloud, but now that they were in the open, I couldn't take them back. "I'm just an orphan girl from a decaying city. How can I do anything to change the world?" *At least no one can say I'm overly confident, right?*

"The smallest movement can shift the current," Professor Berlin's voice was serious and deep. My lips curled into a smile. I liked this eccentric old man.

"Okay," I said. "What do I need to do?"

Chapter 11

∞

I wouldn't be going to the university where the professor taught. Alister had arranged for me to stay at the house here instead. Without a tracker, and no family to speak of, I'd draw too much attention to myself. Until Alister was sure he could find a way to clear my name and put The Nocere mess behind us, both men agreed it was best that I stay hidden.

The old stone building was vast. The marble floored grand room entrance held ancient paintings enclosed in glass. The canvas was so faded on most of them that it was hard to make out the image. This gave the building the sense of dignified respect. I tried to tiptoe past them so as not to disrupt their sleep.

One of the paintings with curling edges displayed an old and knotted tree. I thought of Juniper and my heart ached for the village I'd left behind. I sent up a silent wish to Vorie that she'd check on them for me.

Double doors off the main room creakily opened into a dusty library. Metal bookshelves were installed in front of the crumbling wood ones. Large volumes were stacked unevenly high on the table in the center of the room. I pictured the professor conducting research and leaving these discarded as he carried the rest to his office. Silently scolding him for his carelessness, I ran my finger over the titles. I was surprised to discover a fiction section.

"Does this make you happy?" Alister asked as he leaned against the doorframe.

"More than you know." I smiled as I joined him for the rest of the tour.

Outside the back door was an enclosed courtyard. A dirty and broken water fountain sat in the middle of intricately carved stone benches. Towering trees casting shade grew between walls of ivy and overgrown bushes. The flora was bent on reclaiming the oasis and it made it hard to navigate the walkway.

"In the spring," Alister said, directing my attention to a few trees with barren branches, "These will bloom with cherry blossoms."

I nodded my head slowly as I took it all in. "Do you think I'll still be here in the spring?"

"I hope so," he smiled tenderly. "I hope you'll always want to be here."

"I mean right here." I rolled my eyes. "How long do you think it will be before I'm allowed to leave? I want to check on Brayson at some point and I'd like to get in touch with Genie again."

"I'm working on it." He held out his arm to lead me back to the building. "Come with me. I want to show you your room."

We walked up the grand staircase and turned right down the hall. Alister pushed open a heavy ornate door with cast iron hinges. The windows were left open and the breeze blew against the curtains. Inside the room was a heavy dark wood dresser, a matching wardrobe, a vanity table with mirror, and a large white velvet chair you could lay down on. Near the far wall sat an enormous four poster bed. I ran my fingers over the comforter. It was the same color of sea green as the one I'd left back home.

"How did you have time to do all of this?" I turned to him in confusion. "You only had a moment's notice when I called."

"I was hoping to convince you when I came to visit," Alister shrugged. "I wanted to have it ready just in case. There are a few items in the closet and drawers. I'll bring more the next time I come."

"Are you leaving now?" I looked longingly at the bed, suddenly aware of how exhausted I was.

"Not if you don't want me to." His words were taunting.

I shivered as I crossed my arms over my chest. "I think I need to rest."

"Of course," he said, the playfulness fading from his voice. "I'll be back tomorrow." He walked over to where I stood and placed a gift box on the bed. "It's not much," he grinned as I eyed it skeptically. "We never got the chance to discuss music, but it's loaded with songs that I like. I figured you must be missing your earbuds by now."

I thanked him and he delicately kissed my cheek before leaving the room. The warmth from his lips lingered as I crawled onto the bed. I pulled the soft comforter over me and adjusted the pillows to surround my head. My breath was shaky and uneven as hot tears rolled down my face.

I'd always felt somewhat alone, but I took for granted how much I leaned on my friends. They were the only family I had. Without them, and in a world far away from everything I knew, I felt small sitting on the giant bed. The relaxing ebb of sleep finally overtook me, and I drifted into a dreamless slumber.

*

I woke up starving the next morning. Shaking off the pitiful feelings from last night, I resolved to make the most out of my situation. *See Vorie, I did learn something from you.*

The vanity table held a silver brush. My eyes watered as I yanked it through my wind knotted hair. It seemed as though the events of the day before happened a lifetime ago, but it was only yesterday.

The wardrobe held two tight fitting black dresses. I grimaced when I saw them and slowly backed away. In the dresser drawer, I found a stack of brightly colored lace underwear. *Real cute, Alister.* That man had no idea what I liked.

After making myself as presentable as I could wearing my own dirty clothes over bright purple panties, I crept out of my room and down the staircase. The converted kitchen was near the back door. I smelled food cooking and quickened my steps.

"What are you doing in here?" A woman with curling hair coming out from her loosened braid and a faded apron stretched over her wide hips raised a wooden spoon in my direction. I wasn't sure if I should be afraid, so I took a tentative step back towards the door.

"I smelled food and I'm starving," I stammered. "What can I do to help?"

The woman scrunched her nose as she scowled. "You're a weird one, aren't you? I presume you're the guest of the professor. Breakfast isn't ready for another hour. You're up very early."

I glanced out of the kitchen window. Birds were dancing on the bushes in the courtyard and the sun peaked over the buildings. My forehead creased as I returned her stare.

"What time does the professor normally wake up?"

"When breakfast is ready." The woman returned to stirring the pot on the stove. My stomach growled loudly as I stood there in the doorway. She took pity on me and pulled a weirdly sweet biscuit from the basket. "Here. Eat this." I thanked her as I sat in the chair and finished the biscuit in two bites.

"Are you sure I can't help?" I lingered in my seat. "I'm not sure what else I'm supposed to do."

"I don't know what they do either," the woman laughed scornfully. "But my job is a good one and I'm not about to be replaced."

"I'd never try to take your job." My eyes opened wide at the accusation. "I'm just accustomed to working for my own food." The woman set down her spoon and thoughtfully crossed her arms as she looked me over once more.

"Sweet child," she finally said. "You are going to have a difficult time here. I don't know if we've ever had a guest who has had a day of hard work in their life. My name is Freida. Sit for a while. Tell me where you're from. You can keep me company while I cook."

*

After she'd finished cooking, Freida shooed me into the next room. It was a grand dining hall with a table long enough for twenty guests. The high back chairs were cold and hard, nothing like the worn chairs with patterned cushions in Mrs. Shaw's kitchen. I did my best to ignore the feeling of homesickness as I took the chair to the right of the professor. His books were sprawled across the table and his spectacles were perched on his nose.

"Good morning, sir." I gave him my warmest smile. He looked up as though I'd startled him and glanced briefly at the empty chairs across the table before directing his gaze to me. It suddenly hit me that I wasn't meant to sit this close, but I was already there and didn't feel like moving.

Freida carried in trays of food. Eggs, potatoes, ham, a basket of those biscuits she'd given me, plus more coffee and real milk. Professor Berlin didn't acknowledge her as she entered, but he reached into the basket after she left so he must have noticed that she'd come. Although I thought it was rude, I didn't want to say anything to embarrass my host on the first day.

"I've never had biscuits so sweet," I said as he took a bite of the pastry.

Professor Berlin sipped his coffee before he replied. "They are called scones."

"Hmm," I murmured as I swallowed a mouthful of food. "That's an interesting word. Where are the farms that you get your milk and eggs from?" It was too quiet with just the sound of us chewing, I needed to hear someone else speak. I almost wanted to carry my plate back to the kitchen with Freida, but I didn't want to break any more rules.

"You are peculiar." Professor Berlin raised an eyebrow.

"I could say the same thing about you," I shrugged, causing the old man to laugh.

"Why would you be interested in farms?" He delicately wiped his lips with his napkin before placing it back on his lap. I stared at my untouched napkin on the table.

"I worked on a farm for the past few months," I explained as I slid the utensils off the cloth and placed it on top of my legs. The professor carefully studied me.

"I worry this life will be too hard for you," he said sadly. "Are you sure this is what you want?" His question confused me.

"I don't know what life you are referring to. If someday I can find a way to help humanity like we discussed, I will. For now, I am only here to learn."

"And learn you shall." The professor smiled brightly. "Come to my office at 1 o'clock sharp today." He suddenly scooped up his books in one arm while grabbing his coffee with the other before rushing out of the dining hall. His food sat untouched on his plate. It may not have been my finest moment, but I did eat his piece of ham.

*

After Freida scolded me for carrying the dishes to the kitchen, I wondered aimlessly around the building. I decided it would be less lonely if I was reading so I made my way to the library. The fiction section held mostly ancient texts, but I did find a few I'd never read. The books were caked in dust. I figured no one would mind if I borrowed a few so I gathered some books by forgotten writers to carry to my room.

"There you are, little deer." Alister was standing on the staircase holding bags in his hands. "I was just about to head to your room to drop these off."

I eyed the bags warily. "Not more dresses I hope."

His face dropped in disappointment. "You didn't like them? They reminded me of the ones you wore at Dives."

"They are lovely," I sighed. I truly didn't want to hurt his feelings. "But I'd probably only wear them on a night out."

"You're in luck then," he winked. "I grabbed you some more practical items."

"Thank you," I smiled graciously. "I need to find a way to pay you back for all of this."

"Don't be silly." Alister continued climbing the stairs and I followed him. "There is more than enough here to go around. It isn't like that village you were at."

His words frustrated me, but I bit my tongue. For once, I didn't have anything to say. *Well, anything nice to say.*

He set the bags down on the dresser. "I've missed you. How is everything? Are you comfortable here?" The missing me part caught me off guard. I kind of missed him too.

"You can stay if you want," I laughed. "It seems like I'm not going anywhere."

"I wish I could. There's a trip I need to take, but I should be back within the next week." My breath caught in my throat. I wasn't expecting him to abandon me here.

"Don't worry, little deer." He crossed the room in two long steps to stand right next to me. "It's a quick business thing and I'll be able to figure out how to get the mafia off your tail once I speak to these men."

"Okay," I whispered. Standing this close to him was jarring. I was torn between wanting to grab him and wanting to run away. He wrapped his arm around my lower back, preventing the second option.

"I don't want to leave you," he whispered against my hair. I placed my hand on his chest. The crisp material of his shirt splayed over the beating of his heart beneath my palm.

"I don't want you to leave either." I rolled one of his shirt buttons beneath my finger. He slid his free hand up my waist and along my neck before tilting my face up to his. My brain turned to mush, and I wanted to drown in what was about to happen.

"Stop," I said firmly, although my body screamed in anguish at the word. He paused, breathing heavily, with his lips inches from mine.

"Why?" The question came from somewhere deep in his chest.

I forced myself to take a step back. "We aren't on even footing. You bring me gifts, but I have nothing for you. Plus, I don't want to sleep with you right before you leave me."

Alister smiled. "I know something you can give me as a gift."

"I'm not that kind of girl." I narrowed my eyes.

"Maybe when I get back?" he asked.

"Maybe."

"I'll take a maybe." His green eyes sparkled mischievously.

*

We spent the rest of the morning at a safe distance from each other in my room. Alister's favorite music was instrumental. He preferred the various notes and worked hard to point them out for me. I found a few classic rock songs hidden deep within a playlist. He said he didn't mind them and promised to look for music more to my taste. I thought about bringing up Roger's whisper the night at The Nocere, but we were having too much fun. *I'll wait until he gets back from his trip.*

I also didn't bring up the soulmate conversation because I wanted to learn more about it first. I did spend our time together making a mental checklist of all the things we had in common. Surprisingly, there weren't many. I'd have thought that soulmates would be more in tune with each other. The more we talked, the closer I did want to get to him. I realized it was probably a good thing he was leaving for a while. I needed time to process my feelings before I got carried away.

Freida dropped off lunch in my room for me and my 'visitor'. I could tell by the way she glanced over my shoulder as I thanked her that she wasn't too keen on the situation.

"If she is a problem for you, let me know," Alister spoke seriously as I carried over the tray.

"Why would she be a problem?" I took a large bite of the prepared sandwich. "She's the most comforting part of this whole house."

After lunch, Alister said his good-bye as he walked me to the professor's office.

Chapter 12

∞

Alister and Professor Berlin spoke in hushed tones before he left.

"You know I'm here, right?" I anxiously asked as I sat down in the chair.

"I'd never be able to forget. I'll see you soon." He kissed my cheek as he hurried out the door.

"What was that all about?" I asked the professor. He waved his hand absentmindedly.

"Boring business. Pay it no mind." He folded his hands beneath his chin. "Now, where do we start?"

"You promised to tell me more about the world. Why don't we start there?" I suggested.

"All in good time," he smiled. "Let's start with a game instead. I want to learn more about you and at the end of the game I'll give you a history lesson."

"Okay," I shrugged. "What kind of game?" Professor Berlin clapped his hands together, reminding me of Genie when she got excited. I pushed away the painful memories of her not coming with me as he began to speak.

"I'm going to ask you a series of questions and write down your responses. Please answer truthfully and do not tame your emotional reactions. Are you ready?"

I nodded. The game sounded easy. If there is one thing I'm good at, it's speaking my mind.

"What do you think of Alister?" The professor lifted a yellow notepad and pen from his desk.

"I'm honestly not sure. He is really attractive, and I feel a subconscious pull to him, but I haven't had time to think about it."

"I see." He scribbled some notes and then continued, "Did you enjoy your time on the farm?"

"I enjoyed the whole village," I smiled fondly. "But yes, I enjoyed working on the farm. Everything was so alive. They lived by the sweat of their backs and their own hands. They carved out a life for themselves in this world. I've never felt so at peace as I did while working there."

"Fascinating." The professor returned my smile. "And what is the funniest moment you can remember from your life?" My thoughts instantly went to Genie with her animal print leggings and wild hair. Except, it was more than that.

"I have a thousand funny memories with my friends. Genie in particular. She was such a comedian when we were young. When we were seven, she dropped a basket of rubber snakes into the director's shower. He screamed bloody murder as he ran down the corridor in nothing but his shower cap and wet towel. We laughed until our sides ached," I giggled as I remembered his face again.

"And what about your other friend? The one who was murdered." He didn't join in on my laughter. Instead he scribbled away on the pad.

"Vorie." I lost my smile. "Her name is Vorie. She is the best person in either this world or the realm."

"And how did you feel when she died?" He kept his eyes on the paper.

"Sad," I whispered. "Disappointed really. She wanted to do so many things. She wanted to live, and he took that away from her. Vorie is beautiful. She deserved so much more than what happened."

"And how do you feel about the man who took everything away?"

I blinked hard to stop the tears from falling. The roar of the flames and rage I felt upon seeing the monster filled my mind instead. "I hope his soul burns for all eternity."

Professor Berlin looked taken aback. "You and I both know that isn't possible."

"But if it were, that's what I'd want. That monster is a depraved and heartless being. I hate him." The blood in my veins boiled as I spit out the words.

"Isn't it true this was all your fault though? The man never would have killed Vorie if it wasn't for you." My eyes dropped to the ground as his sentence pierced my heart. The room was beginning to close in.

"It's true," I said quietly.

"And how does that make you feel?"

*

I tuned out the rest of his questions, giving automatic answers. Somewhere in the middle of the conversation he switched topics. I vaguely heard the explanations about what the world was like before the portals, but it no longer mattered to me. My enthusiasm was replaced with an aching weight. There was an anxious fog clouding my mind and the droll of his repetitive voice barely made it through.

Freida announced it was time for dinner. In my dreamlike state I forced my feet to move down the steps and into the dining room. After picking at my food, I mustered the courage to excuse myself so that I could climb into my giant bed. Memories of Genie and Vorie played behind my closed eyelids in a broken loop.

"You didn't do anything wrong." Vorie's soothing voice spoke into my ear as I finally drifted off to sleep. *It sure feels like I did.*

*

When I awoke the next morning, the sun was already turning the world light grey outside my window. I resolved yet again to have a better day and got quickly dressed before heading downstairs. The building was eerily quiet except for the sounds of my shoes tapping against the stone floors.

I made my way into the courtyard. The air had a refreshing new day crispness to it and the birds were beginning to ruffle the dew from their feathers. I stared at the mess of overgrown weeds for a moment before deciding to get to work.

*

"Breakfast is ready," Freida called from the open doorway. I tucked a sweaty piece of hair behind my ear and wiped my dirt stained hands on my pants. The overgrown holly bushes left tiny cuts in my fingers as I'd ripped them back, but the walkway from the fountain to the door was cleared.

Freida stood with her arms folded over her aproned chest. "You'll need some better tools," she said as I walked into the building. "I'll see what I can find."

I sat across the table at the furthest seat away from the professor and gratefully wolfed down the food Freida had prepared. Professor Berlin stood up to leave after finishing his coffee.

"I'll see you in my office this afternoon," he said with his nose buried in the book he carried. I gathered up all our dishes and took them into the kitchen despite the scolding eye of Freida.

Outside the door on the freshly cleared walkway a pair of gloves, a set of sheers, and a trowel lay waiting for me. I called out my thanks to Freida and heard her mumble something back as she busied herself with the housework.

The sun was blazing high in the sky by the early afternoon. The hot air was so sticky I could cut it with a knife. I guzzled some deliciously cool water and then climbed the stairs to the professor's office.

His nose wrinkled as I entered. "You are allowed to shower here."

"Good to know," I smirked as I sank into the chair.

"What have you been doing all day?" He reached for the yellow notebook.

"Working."

"On what?" He adjusted his spectacles and poised his pen above the page.

"On clearing the courtyard."

"And why would you do that?"

"Because it makes this place more livable and while I work, I'm able to process my thoughts better. Heck, if I work hard enough, I don't have to think at all."

"What thoughts do you need to process?" The pen lowered as he got ready to write.

I sighed and leaned my head back against the chair. "I needed to figure out why you were being an asshole yesterday."

"And what did you discover?" he laughed.

I closed my eyes. "That you were trying to get an emotional reaction out of me so you can study how I behave. It does seem ridiculous though. It'd be easier to just ask me. I'm very aware of my behaviors, even the stupid ones." I heard the pen cap close and I opened my eyes. Professor Berlin sat grinning at me.

"That's my theory too."

"What theory?"

"I believe that you have the uncanny ability of self-awareness which affords you a certain characteristic and emotional balance. You feel things so strongly. Yet you are able to manage each feeling in an extraordinary way."

"You might have to dumb that down for the orphan girl."

"Here," the professor chuckled. "Come see this."

I reluctantly stood from the comfortable chair and crossed over to his side of the desk. Mounds of books lay open at different chapters. Religious symbols, words in various languages, psychology and philosophy textbooks, and self-help books all blurred in a kaleidoscope of scattered information.

"This makes about as much sense as your last statement." I glanced over at him. His laughter subsided in a coughing fit. I brought him a glass of water and he slowly regained his breath.

"Start here." He lifted a passage titled *Enlightenment* to the top of the stack.

"What does it mean?" I asked as I skimmed over the words.

"Before we had the portals, there were worldwide centuries old varying beliefs on what happened once we died. Turns out they were all right and also all wrong. We know the afterlife is eternal and this plane of existence, these human bodies, are temporary. Once this ultimate question was resolved there was not much left to live for."

"There is life itself," I shrugged. "Maybe that should be enough."

He gave me a sad smile. "Unfortunately, for most of us that isn't. The old ones used to believe that self-awareness and balance made a person enlightened or a version of their highest self. It seemed they spent years studying how best to live. Now that we have this knowledge their ideas just gather dust. Why waste your lifetime on this plane when eternity awaits?"

"Why are you still here then?" I asked.

"These." He spread his hands out over his work. "I need to keep learning as long as I can. I won't be able to take these with me." He lifted a heavy leather-bound book and dropped it with a loud thud back onto the desk. "But I can take the knowledge with me and I can manifest these books when I get there if I know the contents."

"What you are telling me is that life here in the world is important for multiple reasons." I nudged his shoulder with mine.

"You are a fascinating creature." The professor shook his head. "I can see why Alister is going through all this trouble. Look here." I turned my eyes to where he pointed. "This is a subject we are still working to understand. Magic."

"Fairy tales." I rolled my eyes. He didn't notice.

"Exactly. We'd always believed it was pseudoscience, but the more we learn about energies in the realm, the more we learn about energies in general. It's been proven, as you saw at The Nocere, that certain symbols can have power based on the energy they emit. We know that living creatures all produce their own energy, but we are learning that this energy can be controlled or manipulated in both the world and realm."

"Is that how Fergus can crush a manifestation he didn't create with his own hands?"

Professor Berlin's eyes widened. "You need to stay away from destroyers. Their energies are extremely volatile, and they cause damage wherever they go. It was my understanding that the mafia revokes their trackers and they are placed in some sort of clinical treatment therapy to help control the anger."

"Well I destroyed The Nocere," I shrugged. "Does that make me dangerous?"

"Not in the traditional way," he said softly. "Even a normal destroyer with years of education couldn't dissolve the work of multiple people in the blink of an eye like you did. Alister tells me you are also a truth seeker, that you can see through the glamour. I'm willing to bet you have many other talents waiting to be explored."

"Hang on a second." I walked back over to my chair and sat down rubbing my temples. "Are there other people like me? There has to be, right? People who have more than one talent as you call it."

"I've never met one until now," he said. "There have been rumors and we know of them so I assume there must be. Except there is so much about the realm and our experience in it that we don't know. When the portal technology was released to the general public it went too fast. It wasn't properly studied. Then millions of people left, abandoning all hope of fully researching it. They said there was no need. We'd found out what happens when the human body dies, and the consensus was to not wait any longer when life doesn't matter."

"And how would studying the realm change anything?"

"We could have learned more about ourselves and what that meant not only for the individual but for the collective realm experience. We could have made the realm even better instead of being stuck for all eternity with the limited knowledge we have."

"I'd be lying if I didn't say most of this was going over my head." I gave him a helpless smile.

"I can teach you what I know," he chuckled. "It's what I'm good at doing."

"I'd sure hope so," I laughed. "Not to be self-centered, but what does this all mean for me?"

"It means you have a natural ability that supersedes any human or spirit in the realm I know of. This makes you extremely powerful and potentially dangerous there, but also means you will have more in the afterlife than most."

My eyes welled with tears and I stared hard at the floor so they wouldn't fall. "You're basically saying that my destiny is going to the realm."

"Dear girl." Professor Berlin shook his head. "Everyone's destiny is the realm. There is no escaping that. Don't be frightened though, your destiny right now requires you to live and learn as much as you can about yourself. I strongly believe that it is your love of life that makes you so unique."

Chapter 13

∞

With the weekend over, the professor resumed his classes at the university. Our lessons took place after dinner when we talked late into the night over dripping candle wax. During the days, I busied myself with the courtyard. Once the pathway looping around the fountain was cleared, I began pruning and trimming the remaining flora to create my own little garden.

"I only let you in here because I have to come more frequently to make sure you are fed." Freida stood in the kitchen allowing me to peel apples under her watchful eye.

"You don't have to come just for me. I promise I can fend for myself." I smiled tenderly at the woman.

"Psh. I'm not about to turn down the extra pay. My Odan is at the institute. I've been saving his whole life to make this happen."

The love she had for her son was admirable. She'd told me how she'd supported them both by working for the professor. A few years ago, her husband decided to go to the realm full time, leaving his body for her to bury.

"Good riddance," she'd said more than once. "He was a lazy man."

Through her stories and my nightly lectures with the professor I'd come to learn a lot about the area I was living in. It seemed the professor's house was in an empty neighborhood offset from the main city. The cities around here seemed to be faring better than the rest of the country. Washington D.C. held the seat of this mythical government where Alister worked. The Northeast institute, where Odan lived, was higher on the eastern shore and the professor commuted there daily. There was trade in this region as far down as Florida.

The mafia ran the southern states but there was still a strong government presence within some of them. I guess there was a war, or maybe multiple wars, long before I was born. These were territory disputes which settled in a mafia versus government controlled North American continent.

Professor Berlin explained that similar situations had occurred around the globe with governments or monarchies fighting for control against usurpers. I didn't realize how many wars were fought long before my time. I guess wars are won by large numbers of people. Since this was no longer an option, stale mates and alliances formed in back rooms were the new norm.

I didn't care much about the territory disputes. Where I'd grown up on the west coast was run by the mafia and the government let them have it. It was too far away from their central seat to care. What I cared most about was the farming. The Midwest and Southern Canadian farming families were under government control. I couldn't understand why.

The oil fields in Texas seemed neutral. There was a steel plant in Michigan that belonged to the government and a food packaging plant in Virginia that was mafia run. I knew that Craton's family owned the packaging plant and I clung to any information they discussed on it hoping to learn more about Genie. *I really freaking missed her.*

Brayson was safe in the northwest as far as I could tell. Except for the city of Seattle, the majority of that area was a "no man's land" with neither side able to claim it. I pictured Juniper riding her dirt bike across the mountains and helping the town to work together. They didn't need any of this.

The orphans were hot commodities in the realm, working for both mafia and government sponsored business. When I asked the professor why the mafia runs the orphanages, he told me they don't mind dealing with "those types of people".

"What types of people?" I glared at him, ready to defend my childhood.

"The kind that want to get paid for bringing life into this world," he answered absentmindedly as he flipped through the pages in his book. "They offer those poor souls a large amount of credits in exchange for the child. Whereas the government brings extra food to its citizens' mothers."

"So, the government is the good guy?" I looked down at my hands, grateful he hadn't noticed my reaction.

"Not necessarily. They want the power just as much. They just play their games behind closed doors while the mafia is out in the open." The professor yawned and wished me goodnight. I blew the candles out in his office before heading to my room.

*

"Have you heard anything from Alister?" I skipped into the dining room and pulled out the chair closest to Professor Berlin. "It's been almost two weeks since he left." The professor mumbled something unintelligible as he stared into his cup.

"Let the man drink his coffee before bombarding him with questions," Freida scolded as she set down my plate.

"This looks amazing. Thank you." I smiled up at her. Professor Berlin slowly sipped from his mug.

"Are your magic beans working yet?" I asked as soon as Freida left the room.

"Starting to," he yawned. "Alister has been detained longer than he expected. I thought I told you this a few days ago when he called."

"You did not." I stared at him aghast. "Why didn't you let me speak to him?"

"It was at the university. I don't keep a phone here." He reached for one of his books, but I wasn't letting him off that easy.

"How do phones work anyway?" I folded my arms over my chest.

"We have generators for the cell phone towers and satellites that the signals bounce off. Depending on where you are at you will have phone service." He drained the rest of his coffee cup.

"I have no clue what any of that means. I'm asking how they work. Can I just call anyone I want?"

He gave me the sad smile I'd grown accustomed to anytime I asked a question he thought ridiculous. "Generally, yes. If you have a phone and they have a phone, then you can call them."

"Fascinating," I mimicked his favorite word causing him to chuckle. "Could I have a phone? If Genie is with Craton, she might have one too. Plus, I can call Alister whenever I want."

"That won't be possible." The professor hastily gathered up his books. "Working phones are hard to come by and very expensive. You also don't know Genie's phone number so you wouldn't be able to contact her."

"Ah. I see," I said softly. "Well it would have been a good idea."

"Yes, it would." Professor Berlin gently patted the top of my head before walking to his office.

*

"It feels like it's been forever since he's been gone," I whined to Vorie a few nights later as we sat cross-legged on my giant bed. "Can't you use your all-seeing eye to tell me what's happening?"

"It doesn't work like that," Vorie giggled. "It's not like I know everything. I can focus on you, Brayson, and Genie to see what is going on in your lives because I'm close to you. I don't know Alister well enough to track him down."

"Ugh. What good is having a spirit friend?" I sighed. "How is Genie anyway? Did you tell her I want to see her?"

Vorie's smile faded. "She's getting married soon and has been busy with the preparations."

"Does she need me to help with anything? Oh, I bet she is going nuts over the dress," I laughed but Vorie's face remained stoic. "I'm not invited, am I?"

"Not necessarily. She didn't say no, but she is still so angry with you that she refuses to talk about it."

"If I could just speak with her, I know I could make things right." I hugged the pillow to my chest.

"Why don't you write her a letter and ask Freida if she will find someone to deliver it," she suggested.

"Oh! That's a good idea, but I'm sure it'll be easier for the professor to find a way to get it there." I rummaged through the bedside table to find a paper and pen.

"Trust me on this one," Vorie smiled. "Ask Freida. The professor is so absentminded it will never get there in time if you give it to him."

*

Freida took the letter full of my gushing apologies home with her the next day. She knew a man who delivered to the packaging plant and would see if he could bring it there. I was shocked to learn that we were only a five-hour drive apart. I was really hoping it'd get there in time because I just couldn't miss her wedding. Genie must have been feeling so lonely and I hated that I was the reason for that. When Freida returned in the morning, she said the driver would deliver it that very day. I sent up a silent thanks to Vorie for the great advice.

*

The days were getting cooler, not by much, but I could sit comfortably outside in the afternoon shade. I made a hammock from a sheet and strung it up between two elm trees in the courtyard. The garden was my favorite place and I carried my books outside to read whenever I could.

Swinging under the full branches with the sun peeking through and listening to the melody of the chirping birds, I let the words of Tolstoy lull me into a dreamy daze.

"Count Vronsky was a weak character. I'll never understand what Anna saw in him."

"Alister!" I ungracefully jumped out of the hammock. "You're back! What the hell happened to your face?" He reached up and caressed the fading bruise on his cheek.

"Politics," he shrugged. "Don't worry about it." Every part of me wanted to grab him and the urgency was overwhelming.

I clung to the novel in my hands. "The Count was a side player. Anyone would have done for the role. The story is Anna's alone... Why didn't you get in touch with me while you were gone?"

"I told the professor to let you know I'd be delayed."

"Yes," I nodded. "And he forgot to let me know until I reminded him about it."

"What does it matter? I'm here now. I've missed you, little deer." I missed him too, but I was suddenly so frustrated that I didn't want to admit it.

"You come back with bruises and a simple excuse of being detained. Please explain to me what happened to keep you away." Alister bit his lip smiling as he stepped forward. I took a step back.

"I wouldn't have stayed if I could have helped it." He lowered his eyes to the ground. "It took longer than I expected, but the mafia will no longer bother you."

I breathed a sigh of relief. "Am I free to leave?"

"Not exactly." When he looked up to me his eyes were a mixture of emotions I couldn't read. "My aunt is here. She wants to speak with you."

"Your aunt?" I remembered with vague detail the first night at The Nocere. The woman with the low-cut blouse and scowling eyes. A vodka and tonic. I'd foolishly thought she needed help. *He wants me to meet his family…* I looked down at my tanned bare legs. My knees were scuffed and scabbed from the work in the courtyard.

"Do I have time to change?"

"Yes." He smiled mischievously. "Would you like some help?"

"I'll be just fine. Thank you." I rolled my eyes and started walking toward the door.

"Did you do all this?" Alister asked as he hurried to match my stride. I nodded. "Fascinating." He looked in awe at the work that I'd done, and I laughed to myself thinking of how he'd picked up that word.

Freida was busy in the kitchen and I blew past the entrance as I rushed up the stairs with Alister following me.

"Wait out here." I put my hand against his chest feeling it rise and fall beneath my fingers.

"You shouldn't touch me," he exhaled. "Not after I've been away this long, and not when you won't let me in."

"Wait," I calmly said the word as I saw the fire blaze in his eyes. "I need to find something to wear."

After settling on a nice pair of jeans and simple top, I quickly pleated my hair. My fingernails were chipped from the work in the courtyard, but I wouldn't be able to fix them in time. I took a steadying breath before opening the door. Part of me expected Alister to still be leaning against the frame like he was when I closed the door in his face. He surprised me by standing casually at the top of the stairs.

"Something is different about you, little deer." He extended out his arm to escort me.

"Really? What?" I laced my arm through his and smiled at the tension radiating between us. It was comforting and exhilarating all at the same time.

"I can't put my finger on it yet, but I'm anxious to discover what it is."

Freida ran into the hallway. "Oh good." She placed a shaking hand over her heart. "You're dressed and somewhat presentable. Get to the dining hall. Dinner will be served soon."

"Do you need help in the kitchen?" I worriedly asked her. It was earlier than we normally ate, and I wasn't sure if she'd had enough time to prepare.

"Goodness no." She shooed me away with a dishrag.

Alister laughed as he guided me down the hall. "Maybe you're not so different after all."

Chapter 14

∞

"Here is the little woodland creature that has been causing all this trouble." Alister's aunt stood behind a chair at the dining room table. She looked different than the first night I'd seen her at the club. With her suit jacket buttoned high and her wavy blond hair pulled into a severe bun, she seemed every bit the image of a politician that I'd only ever read about. Her face still held the same scowl though, that part didn't change.

"Trouble?" I mouthed the word to Alister as he pulled out a chair for me.

"No trouble at all," he whispered while casting a disapproving look to his aunt.

"It's nice to see you again," she continued. "You don't look the same without the antlers."

"Fawn," I said, holding out my hand to shake hers across the table. Professor Berlin was sitting in his normal seat watching the scene through his spectacles. Two serious looking men stood at either side of Alister's aunt. The bald one I recognized from the night at The Nocere.

"Of course, we haven't been formally introduced." She placed her icy cold hand in mine and squeezed firmly. "My name is Marley Macavay."

She released my hand and I held it there awkwardly in midair before quickly dropping it to my side. *What did she just say?* My mouth went dry and I swallowed hard. *This can't be right,* my brain screamed. *What the hell do I do?*

I glanced nervously to Alister and then toward the professor. *The flames at The Nocere... Vorie's smile... The spirit of Roger whispering his final words in my ear... The gaping wound on the back of his freaking head!*

"I thought Marley was a man's name," I suddenly blurted out and then clasped my hand over my mouth.

Marley's scowl grew deeper. "She is a weird one, isn't she? I was hoping she'd be less skittish by now. Are you sure about her Professor Berlin?"

I quickly turned to see him nodding. *The professor cannot be in cahoots with this woman.* My thoughts were jumbled and racing. *Is Alister too? Do I say something right now? If they are all involved and I let them know that I know, this could end up bad.* I took a steadying breath as I slowly sat in my chair. My heartbeat was pounding so loud in my ears that I was shocked no one else could hear it.

"Are you alright?" Alister whispered as Freida carried in the trays of food. "You look like you've seen a ghost."

Seen one? I wanted to shout. *More like heard one and I wish that had never happened. Now I can't trust anyone in this room!*

Pure muscle memory plastered a pleasing smile across my face. The smile I'd used my whole life in the realm. "I'm fine," I said softly. "Just a little lightheaded. I think I need to eat something."

After the first course was finished, Marley leaned back in her chair and cast her cold gaze upon me again. "I understand that you and Alister are matched in some way or another. While I can't pretend to understand that, I can understand that my nephew got himself into quite a predicament in order to get the mafia to dismiss your contract and leave you alone. The settlement to this agreement involved a large vat of territory and now I need to know if you are worth it."

"Auntie." I heard the warning in Alister's tone. "It was mine to give, and as I said this doesn't concern you."

"Oh, but it does." Marley's eyes sparkled with hate as she crossed her arms. "As president of this country, it is my sworn duty to protect its citizens from threats."

President? I gulped. *Of course this is happening. I'm seriously in some deep shit right now. Maybe I can fake a headache...*

"Fawn is not a threat." Alister growled beside me.

Right? My mind screamed. *You guys are the threats!*

"I agree with the boy," Professor Berlin chimed in. "She is not a threat and I will personally vouch for her."

"Excuse me?" I cleared my throat as I looked up from the knot of wood on the table my eyes were fixated on. "Why would you think I'm a threat?"

"Threat. Liability. Whatever you want to call it," Marley sighed. "What you did at The Nocere is unheard of. I need to know that you can maintain yourself. When I'd learned an employee, an orphan nonetheless, somehow destroyed the entire structure I sent scouts to find and neutralize you." I felt the color drain from my face as I remembered the two government officials that showed up at the village.

"I can control it," I said weakly. "But it is only a problem in the realm. I don't have a tracker anymore so there is no need to worry."

"Unfortunately," Marley raised a perfectly shaped eyebrow. "You are no good to me here in this plane. You will need a new tracker so I can find out exactly what makes you so special."

"No." An unreal amount of bravery steadied my voice. "I am not going back to the realm."

Alister laid his hand over mine. "I told you Auntie, now is not the time to make any demands." I watched Marley's eyes blaze in outrage before a calm resolution settled over her features.

"In time then," she said coldly as she glanced at our conjoined hands. "Explain to me what this soulmate business entails." The disgust in her voice hit me hard as she turned to face the professor. I pulled my hand into my lap. Professor Berlin gave Alister and I a warm smile. This was a question I hadn't yet asked so my curiosity got the better of me, even though every fiber of my being was screaming for me to get away from these people.

"The soulmate connection is fascinating." Professor Berlin lit up as he spoke. "The theory is that these souls are connected on a very basic molecular level and they are always destined to intertwine. There is an instant connection, a soul recognition if you will," he chuckled at his own bad joke. Marley's blank stare forced him to continue.

"I digress," he coughed. "Their souls will always be tied to each other. They can feel each other in the realm because of the link. They can travel through time and space together because the soul merges when they are close." I looked down at the knot on the table again. This wasn't something I was ready to hear, especially in the presence of a murderous bitch who obviously hated me.

"What does this mean for Alister?" Marley's voice was sharp.

"That is the complicated part," the professor sighed. "Previous theory was that a soulmate connection was two halves of a whole meeting. Modern research has suggested that this is only true in part. Souls are whole entities on their own, but when this connection is discovered, they will be broken without each other."

Great. Well at least I already feel broken most of the time. So, it won't be much of a change when I leave this place and these crazy people. I looked up to the professor's animated face.

"Here is the truly fascinating part," he smiled broadly. "Side by side they enhance each other. Their souls literally ignite with the added strength of being so possessed by another spirit."

"Alister is stronger with you by his side." Marley scornfully studied my face while a cruel grin turned up her lips. "Well little deer, I guess we will need you after all."

"There still is one weakness," Professor Berlin babbled away. "Each other. If something were to happen to or threaten the other's wellbeing, this becomes a weakness leading the other soul to its demise. Then they will only be reconnected in the realm. Which would have happened anyway…"

"What do we do to negate this risk?" Marley interrupted him. The professor's brow creased in confusion.

"We make her stronger," the bald man said, breaking his statue like demeanor. "She needs to be strong enough to enable Alister to fulfill his destiny as president one day."

Um, screw that, I thought as I glanced back at Alister. He narrowed his eyes at his aunt.

"Fawn is stronger than I am already," he growled in a commanding tone. "You will leave her alone." And just like that, I realized I really liked him.

"Excuse me," I said as I put my hands firmly on the table and pushed back my chair. "I've heard enough talk of who I am and what to do with my life without my own input for the evening. Unless there is something you want my opinion on, I see no reason to stay for the conversation."

"You are dismissed," Marley said coldly.

"I didn't need your permission." I matched her smirk with one of my own. As I turned to leave, I heard the professor chuckle quietly.

*

"Wait Fawn." Alister stopped me on the stairs. "I didn't realize she would act that way."

I gripped the banister firmly. "This is a whole lot of stuff that I didn't sign up for. Why didn't you tell me you would be president some day? And why didn't you say your last name was Macavay?"

"You never asked," he shrugged. "And what does it matter? There are supposed to be elections. My family has held the presidency line for generations, but there is always a chance we could get voted out. It isn't set in stone that I will be president."

"Your aunt seems to think that you will," I huffed. "I think I'd like to leave here."

"You can't go," Alister said painfully. "I need you too much."

"To help fulfill your destiny? No thanks." I took the next step.

"No," he said as he raced up the steps. "Because I can't breathe without you." He grabbed me by the hand at the top of the landing. "From the first night I met you, you've been in every one of my dreams. The months you were gone were so bleak. I was desperate to find you. I want you, little deer, and I need you to stay."

The intensity of his gaze and the urgency of his voice tugged at my core, forcing me into his arms. My lips betrayed me as they gently brushed against his. Then suddenly I was drowning, swimming, pulled against the tide of wanting to be nowhere else but this very moment. I didn't realize we were moving down the hall still locked in each other's embrace until he took his hand away from my back to open the bedroom door.

"Stop," I whispered breathlessly. *Don't say that*, my body screamed. "I need time to process this all." Alister stood frozen for a heart pounding second and I watched the torment play across his face.

I took a step into my room. "The stakes are higher now. I need to think, and I can't do that when you are around." He bit his lip before reluctantly turning down the hall. I closed the heavy door, letting out a frustrated and shaky breath.

*

The dusk was beginning to settle in the room and the shadows of the furniture elongated. The lantern wick flickered its tiny flame as I sat cross-legged on top of the bed. I slowly picked at a loose string on the comforter as I repeated the words aloud once more, "I could really use someone to talk to right now. Mind coming to visit me, Vorie?"

"I'm here," she said as she materialized at the foot of my bed. "Sorry it took so long. You wouldn't believe all the stuff you have to learn as a spirit."

I sighed in relief as I looked at my friend. "What kind of stuff are you learning?"

"How to create my own paradise. That's kind of fun. I mean, I know we know how to manifest the small things, but building an entire world takes a lot of effort. Brayson thinks it's neat though. He can't wait to come see it." She moved across the bed until she was sitting beside me.

"Has he been to visit you there?" I asked.

"No." Her face fell for a moment before she quickly donned another smile. "He doesn't want another tracker right now and I agree that's for the best. He is happy in the village. I spend most nights with him there. Genie comes to see me though."

I pulled the string free from the blanket, feeling like a horrible friend. "I don't mean to take you away from him."

"It's fine," she giggled. "He's still at work building a brand-new barn for Fallon with his bare hands. It's kind of sexy."

I laughed despite the overwhelming longing to be back at the village with them. "How is Genie? Did she get my letter?"

"I don't want to ruin the surprise," Vorie winked. "You'll see very soon." My heart leapt at her answer and I resolved to wait patiently.

"Speaking of surprises," I said. "Do you remember what Roger whispered to me the night I burned down The Nocere?"

"I have no idea." Her eyes shifted ever so slightly. "I wouldn't have been able to hear it."

"Bullshit!" I pulled the throw pillow out from between us and tossed it through her ghostly form. "You knew he told me the name of his murderer. Oh Vorie, I'm in some deep crap. What am I supposed to do? And why didn't you warn me she was coming?" Vorie burst into laughter and I sat solemnly while waiting for her to get it under control.

"I didn't know the name," she said after calming down her fit. "That shocked me as much as it did you."

"You know what this means, right?" Angry tears were forming in my eyes. "She killed her running mate and covered it up. Roger made me promise I'd never tell anyone the name, but I almost told Alister. Could you imagine if I had? Why would Roger do this to me? I didn't even know him. Now I'm in a messed-up family situation with people who are no better than the customers at The Nocere. Seriously, what am I supposed to do?"

"Keep doing exactly what you are doing," Vorie smiled. "You are where you are supposed to be. All of this is just building blocks leading to your destiny."

"You know if I hear the word destiny one more time tonight, I'm going to vomit," I glared at her.

"Thankfully, I'm a ghost. I don't have to worry about getting sprayed," she laughed.

"I love you so much you weirdo." I couldn't help but smile. "Alright. What does this destiny of mine entail?"

"That I can't tell you," she sighed. "Just keep being yourself. It will all work out."

*

"I have something for you," Freida called from the door leading to the courtyard. I was in the back-corner clearing some of the underlying brush beneath the cherry blossom trees.

"What is it?" I removed my gloves and beat them against my leg to loosen the dirt from them.

"Come here and get it. I'm not your maid," Freida grumbled as she headed back inside. I raced down the walkway and into the kitchen.

"Go take your shoes off," she scolded. "You're tracking in mud." I hurried to remove my sneakers and carried them back outside.

"What is it?" I anxiously asked as I slid back across the stone floors into the kitchen. She was busy ladling creamed wheat into bowls. I took the pot from her hands to help.

"What is what?" She asked as she moved to pull the muffins from the oven.

"You said you had something for me." I put the pot down and bounced on the balls of my feet.

"Oh that." Freida smiled playfully. "You received a letter from your friend."

"Where is it?" I shrieked.

"I know I put it somewhere." She slowly searched the countertops before patting her apron pocket. "Ah, yes. Here it is." She handed me a thick envelope closed with a red wax seal.

"Thank you so much," I beamed while clutching it to my chest.

"Breakfast is in twenty minutes. Don't be late," she called out after me as I skipped out of the kitchen.

Chapter 15

∞

I sat on the cold stone floor against the marble case displaying a painting enclosed in glass. It was always so quiet in the room that held the artwork of the dead. I anxiously broke open the seal on the letter. The first page was blank except for the single handwritten sentence:

I guess you are forgiven because you asked so nicely.

I quickly tossed the page to the floor beside me as I rushed through the swirling calligraphy of Genie's excitement. Four hastily scribbled pages detailed all that happened since Brayson and I left L.A.

A week after we were gone, Genie had a breakdown in the realm at the tiny cottage Vorie was manifesting. It seemed that Vorie somehow got in touch with Craton and he stayed with her in our flat for a few weeks. He finally convinced her to move to Virginia. She wouldn't have gone if it weren't for Lane coming home to announce he was moving to Brazil with the bouncer he'd met at Dives. I smiled to myself upon reading that. I was happy he'd found someone to love.

Then Craton and Genie drove across the country. It was hard to imagine her camping on the side of the road. She described the desert wasteland and open country in passing descriptions, but she gushed about how well Craton handled driving the decaying highways.

Virginia was rough, but she was learning to manage. There were bustling towns to visit which were so different than where we were from. He always spoiled her in the realm. Craton's parents were another story. They treated her with a distant kindness, but she could tell they didn't approve.

It doesn't matter though because we are getting married!!

I laughed at her unabashed enthusiasm. The final page went over the details of the wedding. She'd found the perfect dress which was custom designed as a gift from Craton. The only thing missing was her maid of honor.

Consider the first page of this letter revoked if you aren't there to walk me down the aisle!

The wedding date was in three days. I hastily folded the letter as I jumped to my feet and rushed into the dining hall.

"Professor Berlin!" I screamed as I slid across the polished floor. "I have to take a trip somewhere. Is there a place nearby that I can get a car? And I'm definitely going to need a road map." I started to jump up and down as I watched him sip his coffee.

"What's all this fuss about?" Freida pointed to a chair and I reluctantly sat in it as she served the food.

"My best friend's wedding is in three days and she is going to kill me if I'm not there." I ripped into a muffin, dropping crumbs all over the table which I quickly swept into my hand before Freida noticed. "She's in Virginia. It's not that far away. I'll just have to find a car."

The professor rubbed his eyes and then stared deeply into his mug. "I'm not sure that is a safe plan. President Macavay thinks you should probably stay hidden a while longer."

"Excuse me?" I set down the remainder of the muffin and placed my hands on the table. "I don't think I'm under the jurisdiction of that woman. It's my understanding that the threat to me has passed. I am going to my friend's wedding."

He raised his tired eyes to look at me. "True, there is no longer a bounty on your head, but there are many people out there who've heard of what you can do. It's safer to stay hidden until we know how to protect you."

"I don't need protection." I returned his stare with my own.

"Now, dear." Freida stood with her hands on her hips. "There is no reason to be snappy, he only has your best interest in mind." I nodded begrudgingly.

"Professor Berlin," she turned to face him. "It isn't natural to keep a young woman locked up in these stone walls forever. Is there any way to outfit her with a security detail so she can attend the wedding?" I felt more than heard the shift in the professor's tone when he addressed Freida. Looking between the two of their faces, I suddenly realized there was more to their relationship than I'd previously thought.

"I'm afraid I'm not authorized to make this decision. Alister will be here later today. We can bring it up with him then. Can I ask how you learned of this affair?" He turned his attention back to me. I felt Genie's letter burning a hole in my back pocket. Freida's ruddy cheeks flushed a deeper shade of red.

"My friend Vorie came to visit and told me about it," I whispered.

"I see," the professor nodded. Freida refilled his coffee cup before bustling out of the room. "My hands are tied on this matter, but you can tell me what you'd like to send for a wedding gift, and I'll make sure to have it delivered."

I numbly pushed the food around in my bowl, watching the birds through the window dance happily in the courtyard.

*

The afternoon lesson covered emotional reaction. We scoured books that discussed allowing feelings to be felt but moving through them and maintaining control. These were things I assumed I already knew, but the professor assured me the study and additional practice was beneficial.

His theory on why I was different than others in the realm was intertwined with his theory on why humanity left in the first place. He found this all, *you guessed it,* fascinating.

It seemed that the reality of an eternal paradise in contrast with a short and miserable life was too much to pass up. According to his theory, in giving up their humanity those in the realm did not ever reach their true human potential. Therefore, they couldn't attain the state of being relative to their highest selves. Basically, people leave this world thinking it's bad and then doom themselves to an eternal state of half existence. I somehow already figured this out without consciously thinking about it. I found that last bit fascinating too.

"I'm learning more from you every day," the professor smiled. "Now I just need to find a way to convince this old brain of mine to change so I can be just like you when I grow up."

"What happens if we are all like her?" Alister asked as he leaned against the doorway. I knocked over a stack of books on the desk as I raced to him.

"Sorry!" I cried as I ran back to pick them up.

The professor chuckled. "Then I suppose we'd no longer have a need for the portals."

*

"Genie's wedding is in three days!" My words came rushing out as I dragged Alister into the hall. "I need to be there and now the professor is telling me your aunt says I'm not allowed to leave." The half smile, half soul crushing pain in his eyes let me know the truth.

"I have to be there," I begged. "Please help me find a way." He sat down on the top step and draped his long arms over his knees as he looked at the foyer below.

"I searched for you," he finally said. "I spent a month searching the back country of Idaho where you said you were going to be. I couldn't find a trace of you anywhere. I'm not sure what I was going to do when I found you, but I was ready to leave all this and stay."

"You never told me that." I sat down beside him and pressed my body against his. Warmth instantly comforted me, and I hoped it felt the same for him.

"I didn't want to worry you or maybe I didn't want you to think I failed." He studied the lines on his hands. "Either way, I didn't find you and I had to come back to my world. That's when I learned there was a price on your head. The inner circles of the elites, as you like to call them, all spoke in hushed whispers of this dangerous orphan girl. They don't know everything you are capable of, and if they did, they would do anything to use you for their own gain."

"If they find out what I can do, would they mind telling me what that is too?" I laughed.

"I'm being serious here," he smiled.

"I know," I said. "But I refuse to live in fear, and I can't abandon my friend again."

"Let me speak to the president," Alister sighed. "I'll see what I can do."

*

I woke early the next morning although I wanted to sleep in. The sun peaked over the buildings surrounding the courtyard and I methodically tugged at the weeds.

"Breakfast," Freida called. I trudged slowly past her into the dining room. The world seemed unsteady, my life on a balance beam, as I waited to hear from Alister.

"You're quiet this morning," the professor remarked as I silently stared at my food.

"Alister is asking his aunt if I can go to Genie's wedding. I can't think of anything else," I shrugged.

"Did you decide on a gift for her?" he asked as he sipped his magic brew. I shook my head no, knowing she'd throw whatever I sent away if I wasn't there to give it to her.

*

I found myself watching the hands of the clock as they slowly ticked toward the afternoon.

"Lesson today?" the professor asked as he passed me on the stairs.

"I'm not sure I can focus," I sighed as I stared at the front door. "Do you mind giving me a rain check?"

*

The minutes turned to hours. The sun set and the candles were lit. I sat on the cold steps and stretched out my aching back.

"Why don't you go to sleep sweetheart?" Freida had taken off her apron and pulled on her sweater. "Tomorrow is another day."

"I have to get to her." My eyes felt bloodshot as I stared at the door, willing Alister to walk through. "You don't understand. She is my family."

Freida thoughtfully watched me for a moment before creeping back down the hall. Her face was resolute when she returned. "Go get your things."

I stared at her in confusion as the weight of her words registered. Then I raced up the stairs to throw a bag quickly together, grabbing one of the black dresses from the hanger to also put inside. I closed the heavy door to my room silently. I'd be lying if I didn't say a part of me never wanted to see it again.

*

Freida kept a finger pressed to her lips as I crept back down the stairwell. Once we were outside, the cool breeze of the night air danced over my skin causing me to shiver. We walked in silence to Freida's car.

"Are you going to get in trouble for this?" I asked her as I fastened the passenger seatbelt around my waist.

"In trouble for what?" She shifted the transmission into drive. "I don't know anything about this. You were sitting on the steps when I left for the night."

I smiled for the first time that day as she maneuvered the car down the city streets. Tall apartment buildings stacked right next to each other lined the road she turned onto. The road was full of commotion as people crowded in the middle. She parked inside a cement garage where thirty or so other vehicles were nestled into painted lines.

When we walked down the steps to the sidewalk, the sound of musicians playing their instruments and the laughter of the gathered people overwhelmed my senses.

"What is this place?" I turned to ask.

"They call it the ghetto," she laughed. "But to me it is home."

"Is it like this all the time?" I watched a woman ladle soup out to a line of hungry unwashed customers. Another man poured strong smelling beer into cups for the line of people at his stand. The balconies above the street held lines of washing being wrung out by women who called to each other as they worked. It reminded me of market day at the village in a sense, yet there were easily triple the amount of people.

"In the warmer months it is." Freida handed over a bag of apples and smiled graciously as she accepted two cups of beer from the distributor. She leaned over to whisper in his ear. The man nodded before we walked away.

"Winters are harsh here," she continued to explain. "Many will leave, but more always come back in the spring. This year has been a mild one, so the neighborhood is full." She ushered me past the crowds and led us up a rickety staircase into her small two room apartment.

"The beer man's name is Porter. He's the one who delivered your letter. He leaves at 5 o'clock in the morning daily to travel to Virginia. He'll take you to your friend's house tomorrow."

"I don't know how I'll ever repay you." I smiled as she handed me a cup.

"Just don't get into any trouble and come right back here when you are done. The upper class is always making mountains out of mole hills. What harm can come from a girl going to her best friend's wedding?"

I slowly sipped the beer, letting the bubbles tickle my lip. Even though I agreed with her, I couldn't shake the feeling that I was about to get in a heck of a lot of trouble.

After she showed me Odan's room, she fixed a bed for me on the sofa.

"I like to keep it the way it is for when he returns," she explained.

"This is perfect," I reassured her.

It was after midnight as I sat in a chair near the window watching the street below. The party had grown louder. People stumbled and danced around fires built in barrels. The amount of life here was inspiring. I felt it'd be terrible to see this place abandoned in the winter.

Freida's boisterous snores coming from her thin bedroom walls reminded me that I should try to sleep. I laid down on the tiny sofa and snuggled under the blanket. My tossing and turning was punctuated by snippets of fractured dreams involving wolf eyes and butterfly wings.

Chapter 16

∞

"It's time to go." Freida stood next to the sofa shaking me awake with one hand and holding a brown paper bag in the other. My eyes burned as I opened them. The apartment was still dark, and it felt like I'd only slept ten minutes.

"What time is it?" I jumped to my feet.

"Time to go see your friend get married." She put the paper bag in my hand. "Here is breakfast for you and Porter. Now hurry down to the street. He'll be waiting for you. I'm going back to bed."

"Thank you so much for everything." I wrapped my arms around her shoulders.

"Go now," she laughed while pushing me away. "And hurry back."

I tucked the food into my bag and rushed down the stairwell. The cold air shocked me alert. My breath came out in short puffs of steam as I stood shivering on the sidewalk. A large truck roared to life at the corner and I saw Porter waving to me from the driver side window. I ran to the vehicle and climbed inside.

"Thank you so much for doing this." I held out my hand. "My name is Fawn. It's nice to meet you."

"I know your name." He released the brake. "No need for pleasantries. Any friend of Freida's is a friend of mine." We drove in silence until the city was behind us. When the sun rose, and I couldn't deal with my stomach grumbling any longer, I dug out the paper bag from my pack.

"Freida made us breakfast," I said, breaking our quiet understanding. "Are you hungry?"

Porter eyed the bag in my hand. "Did she make some of her scones?"

We ate blueberry scones and hunks of cheese as we continued down the worn-out highway. Lines of trees broke into the asphalt. Porter avoided these and the potholes effortlessly.

"Have you driven this road before?" I asked as he gracefully maneuvered around another broken pit.

"Almost every day since I was eighteen," he muttered.

Hours passed but the scenery didn't change much until we saw the cluster of buildings rising over the freeway.

"I'll be leaving this afternoon, but I'll be back in the morning. The wedding is at 10 o'clock tomorrow. I'll pick you up at 4 o'clock right at this spot." Porter slowed the truck and pointed to an empty bench.

"How do you know what time the wedding is?" I pressed my face to the window and studied the landmarks of the area so that I wouldn't forget where to go.

Porter chuckled. "It's all anyone has been talking about for weeks now. An orphan child and a rich son getting married. Why, it's a modern-day Cinderella story."

On the next block, Porter pulled the break and let the truck idle on the street.

"That green door there. That's where your friend is." I looked at the abandoned buildings. Genie's letter described towns bustling with life.

"Are you sure?" I turned to ask him. "She didn't make it seem that she lived this isolated."

"Probably because they didn't want the attention drawn to her," he laughed. "Turned them on their heads it did. This is the place though. She answered the door when I dropped off the letter."

"Okay," I smiled at the man. "I really appreciate you bringing me here. I'll see you at the bus stop tomorrow at 4 o'clock."

"No trouble," Porter blushed. The engine roared to life as he put it in gear and drove away.

For a moment I panicked at being left alone on the seemingly empty street. The little house with the green door was smashed between two large industrial buildings. The shades were drawn tight and the front porch was devoid of any signs that someone lived there. *Why would Porter lie to me?* I shook off the fear and climbed the steps.

"Genie," I called as I dropped the iron knocker repeatedly against the wood. "Are you home?"

There was no answer. I beat the knocker harder in frustration. Just as I was about to turn away, the interior lock clicked, and the door cracked open an inch.

"Oh my God," Genie shrieked as she threw the door wide open. "I can't believe you are actually here!"

Tears sprang into my eyes as she wrapped me in the tightest hug. "Did you think I'd miss your wedding?"

"I didn't know what to think," Genie cried. "After Vorie told me what was going on with you, I just didn't know what would happen. Come in." She dragged me into the house and bolted the door behind her. "Let me look at you!"

Her hair was pinned in soft curlers and she wore a bright pink terry bathrobe. Sleep was crusted in the corner of her eyes.

"Did I wake you?"

"It's okay," she giggled. "I needed to get up anyway. I've been sleeping so late these past few weeks. There is nothing to do during the day when Craton works, but you're here now. We should celebrate."

"I came to celebrate that you're getting married," I laughed. "What do you need me to do to help with tomorrow?"

"It's all been taken care of," Genie shrugged. Her smile slightly faltered. "I didn't get much say in the matter. Craton's mother planned it according to their customs."

I walked across the orange and brown striped carpet to sit on the purple loveseat. "Maybe that's not such a bad thing," I smiled. "Your style is a little loud." Genie rolled her eyes.

"Let her have the wedding reception," she smirked. "When Craton and I move into the big house, I'm redoing it all to my taste. I did get to pick my wedding dress though. Oh Fawn, it's so gorgeous."

"I'm sure it is. I can't wait to see it."

"It's at the big house now, but obviously I'll be able to show you tomorrow. I still can't believe you're here." She jumped onto the couch and hugged me again. "I was so worried I'd have to do this alone."

"Hey. I've been here." Vorie's ghost materialized in the center of the room.

"You know what I mean," Genie laughed. "Maybe we should have just done this in the realm." I glanced nervously at the thick scar on my arm where I'd dug out my tracker twice. Without turning to me, Genie placed her hand on it. "But then Fawn couldn't be there either. This is perfect enough," she declared.

Vorie smiled ear to ear. "I was going to give you two some time alone, but I just couldn't stay away. Tell me we are having a bachelorette party tonight."

Genie's eyes lit up. "Of course we are! Let me just go get ready."

We decided to find wine and get food from the next town over. Then we'd bring it here for a girls' night. Vorie promised to be back by dinner. I dozed off on the couch while Genie got ready.

"Why do you park in the alley?" I asked as we climbed into her gleaming white Mustang.

"So that no one knows I'm here."

I stared at the abandoned buildings we passed. "I don't think there is anyone here to care."

"I could have lived at the big house," Genie sighed. "Craton begged me to. I just wanted to be alone for a while longer until after we were married. I'll probably move there after the wedding. It's just so big and the grounds are huge. They call it a plantation. Everything is green and there are trees everywhere. You are going to love it."

"Why didn't you move to the town then?" I was having a hard time picturing her wanting to be alone.

"It's such a cute little place," she grinned. "But there are too many people. It doesn't feel like home." I sat in silence watching her. She'd changed in the past few months and my heart hurt learning there were things about her I didn't know.

"Remember when you put the snakes in the director's shower?" I suddenly laughed.

"Remember when I had to scrub toilets by myself for a month after that?" she giggled. "It was so worth it. I can still hear those high-pitched screams." She parked in front of a busy marketplace.

"Let's go get the wine first," she said as we walked down a beaten path behind the stalls. The walkway ended at a brick house with white columns. Genie paid with tracker credits for three bottles of wine.

"We'll drink Vorie's for her," she winked. After she stowed the bottles in the trunk of the Mustang, we walked over to the crowded square.

"Have you tried pizza yet?" she asked. I shook my head. "Oh my God, we are getting you some pizza." She looped her arm through mine and dragged me to a delicious smelling stall. Bread pie type things were baking on a stone slab over a fire.

While our order was cooking, I looked at the other shoppers and vendors. This place was organized and vibrant. A grown-up version of the market that Juniper was trying to build. I missed the sleepy village and the Ruby Mountains. I missed the desert browns lightly colored with specks of sagebrush and orange poppies, but this was beautiful in its own way too.

A face suddenly appeared at the end of the square above the heads of the other shoppers. My muscles froze. *Is that Fergus?*

I dropped down behind the pizza vendor's tent and pulled Genie by her leg. "I need to go."

She raised an eyebrow as she took the boxes of food. "Is something happening?"

"I just saw Fergus. Why is he here?" I whispered as I dragged her between the buildings and out into the back alley.

"You're freaked out about Fergus? He's around here sometimes now. He does some work for Craton's father."

"Is he going to be at the wedding?" I frantically asked as we climbed into the car.

"He's not on the guest list." Her forehead creased. "Why are you acting so weird? You worked with him at the club and you knew he works for the mafia. Even Craton has grown to like him, although I don't know why he didn't in the first place. Is Fergus dangerous to you or something?"

"I'm not sure." I bit my lip as we pulled away from the market and back onto the freeway. "I just don't think I'm ready to find out right now."

*

I held Genie's hair back as she threw up into the bucket.

"I told you not to let her drink the second bottle," Vorie sighed.

"As if Genie ever listened to either of us." I glared at her smug spirit face.

"I'm fine," Genie groaned. *She was not fine.* I tried my best to clean her up and forced her to eat another piece of pizza.

"We need to get you to bed," I told her. "Your wedding is in the morning."

"I don't want to go to bed," she cried. "And screw the stupid wedding. I don't even want to get married."

"That's not true," Vorie soothed her. "I've seen you with Craton. You really like him."

"He's alright," Genie burped. "I just hate his whole stupid family. Did you know his dad is some sort of mafia boss? I'm not only sleeping with the enemy. I'm marrying into the family." She began to cry incoherently against her pillow as I rubbed her back.

When I thought she was asleep, I nodded to Vorie and turned off the bedside lamp.

"Fawn," Genie whispered. "Please don't leave me alone."

"I'm right here." I snuggled next to her on the bed. Vorie went back to the realm and I held Genie for the rest of the night.

*

I woke up to the sound of someone knocking on the front door. The bed beside me was empty and cold. Weak light came through the window. *Who the hell is knocking this early?* Panic caused me to sit upright. *What if Fergus saw me?*

"Just a minute," Genie called from the washroom before walking into the bedroom. "Oh good. You're awake. The ride is here a little early."

*

"How do you look this amazing after how much we had to drink last night?" I nursed a headache with sips of water as we sat in the backseat of the van with black tinted windows.

"Practice," she laughed.

"Are you really okay though?" I stared hard at my friend, trying to see through the real-world glamour.

She glanced at the driver and raised her chin. "Why wouldn't I be? I'm the luckiest little orphan girl in the whole world. All my dreams are coming true."

Chapter 17

∞

The cobblestone paved driveway that lead to the plantation home stretched for miles it seemed. Horses galloped in the pastures behind the fences that lined the road and perfectly manicured elm trees decorated the way.

"It's like a fairy tale," I gasped as the old home with the wrap around veranda porch came into view.

"It sure is," Genie's voice was flat. Women in starched black dresses and crisp white aprons ushered us into the house.

"And who is this?" A taunt and darkly feminine older version of Craton met us at the top of the stairs.

"It's my long-lost sister," Genie smiled triumphantly. "Here to walk me down the aisle." Craton's mother let out a *pft* sound as she opened the double doors to the bedroom suite.

Genie sat perfectly still as people busied themselves with her makeup and hair. I sat there awkwardly on the ottoman at the foot of the bed as I watched the parade.

"Do you need anything?" I asked her when the moving bodies of the attendants gave me an opening.

"Champagne would be nice." She motioned with her eyes toward the bar cart. I poured a small amount into a crystal flute. Then on second thought, I filled it the rest of the way.

"Perfect," she smiled gratefully before drinking it in a single gulp despite the scolding of the makeup artist. I took the glass back for a refill and wiped the bright red lipstick from the rim.

"Do we have anything for Fawn to wear?" Genie suddenly asked. I unzipped my bag and pulled out the black dress Alister had left me in the closet. Genie frantically looked about the room.

"That wrinkled old thing?" Craton's mom sneered from her pampering in the corner. "I'm sure we can find your sister something more decent to wear."

Genie's eyes lit up in defiance. "Oh, but it's perfect! I'm sure someone in here won't mind pressing it quickly. After all, I want my sister to feel comfortable on my special day."

The attendants silently looked from the bride to the future mother in law. A brave girl finally stepped forward and took the dress from my hands. Craton's mother grumbled in her corner.

There was a reserved excitement about the room as the wedding dress was carried in. Craton's mother stood with a hand over her heart. I saw Genie's sly wink at the brave girl who'd just returned my freshly pressed outfit. Genie's gown took two attendants to slip it up and tie it to her body.

Craton's mother made a gasping noise that sounded awfully like she was about to faint. She excused herself to get some fresh air. The remaining attendants turned to clap for Genie once the woman left the room.

The gown was floor length with a four-foot train that the attendants spread out delicately on the carpet. Intricate butterflies with burnt wings were embroidered on the bodice and trim. The too tight bodice pushed her breasts up seductively and her bare shoulders received a dusting of gold shimmer. It was elegant and sexy, in the style that only Genie would wear.

"What do you think?" Genie smiled at her reflection in the mirror.

"It's perfect." I clasped her outstretched hand. The exhausted attendants fell away and ran to help with the reception preparations.

The usher knocked on the door just as I got dressed. "It's time," he informed us.

"Wait for me at the bottom of the stairs," Genie instructed.

I paused as I stood next to her. "Are you sure you want to do this? We can run away now if you want. No questions asked. We can just go."

Genie raised her chin and looked determinedly over my head. "Orphans don't get many chances at a good or easy life. I'd be a fool to pass this up. I've made up my mind."

"Okay," I whispered as I smiled at my friend. "I support whatever you want to do."

I stepped silently and unnoticed down the staircase. The foyer turned toward an open ballroom. Chairs were filled on both sides of the room with guests wearing black. I fit right in and laughed to myself knowing how much Genie was about to stand out. The music began and everyone quieted down their chatter.

Genie descended the grand staircase. She looked the perfect part of poise and calm, but when she wrapped her arm through mine, I felt the hurried flutter of her pulse pounding against her skin.

"Breathe," I said, winking horribly at her.

"You breathe too," she smiled.

The guests turned to look as she entered the room. A few of the elderly women whispered to one another as we passed, but in typical Genie fashion, she didn't notice or care.

Craton's smile beamed so bright it lit up the entire room. Tears ran down his cheeks as he stared at her and I felt hope rise in my chest. *If he loves her this much, maybe her life will be a good one.* The ceremony dragged on until the final kiss. I mean, the kiss dragged on too, but the gasps from the gossiping old ladies made it anything but boring.

*

"Hey Fawn." Craton walked up to Genie and me as we walked around the outdoor garden where the simple lunch reception was taking place. "I didn't know you were coming."

"I didn't think she'd make it either until she showed up yesterday on my doorstep," Genie laughed.

"How long are you planning to stay?" Craton nervously wrung his hands as he glanced toward the other guests.

"What's gotten into you?" Genie eyed her new husband. "It's not like she is causing any problems."

"It's alright," I reassured her. "My ride is coming at 4 o'clock near your house. I'll need to leave soon."

"Oh. I'll go get you a driver." Genie gave Craton a long look before heading down the walkway to find an attendant.

"I assume you know what I did?" I asked him once she was out of earshot.

Craton nodded in relief. "We all heard. My father wanted to send his men to hunt you down too, but I assured him you weren't a threat. I don't think anyone here knows exactly who you are, but it's probably best to stay low. Supposedly the government paid a large sum to get the mafia to leave you alone. Except, you aren't in government territory right now."

"I didn't realize you were so high up on the mafia chain," I said quietly.

"I'm not," Craton sighed. "I suppose I'll have to be someday. When I take over ownership of the processing plant in a few years I'll belong to the inner circle of regional bosses, I guess. As long as I do my job, I won't have to take an active role like my father does."

"Craton," a loud voice boomed from the edge of the path. "Please come here. There seems to be a problem."

Genie came flying down the walkway. The hem of her dress and train got snagged on the branches of the hedge bushes. She grabbed my arm and pulled me behind the gazebo as Craton hurried to his father.

"The president is here looking for you," she rushed out the words. "This is really bad. They all hate her. We need to get you somewhere safe. Maybe Fergus can help. I'll take you to him."

"Damn it," I groaned. "I'm in such deep trouble right now. I can't go with Fergus. I need to go with her."

"Are you sure about this?" She raised an eyebrow. "Do you trust that woman?"

"Not if my life depended on it," I smirked. "But I need to go so the rest of your wedding day doesn't get ruined."

"It's okay," Genie smiled. "This party sucks anyway."

We hugged each other tightly and promised to see each other more. Then I crept along the side of the house while she returned to her guests. The long circle driveway was packed with running vehicles blocking the exit. Government guards stood outside on alert.

I heard Marley Macavay's cold voice as she addressed Craton and his father on the porch. Alister leaned against the last vehicle with his arms folded over his chest. Under the open flap of his jacket, I saw the gun holstered on his side.

"Please don't be mad," I said to him as I stepped out from the tree line.

"Fawn," Alister barked. A mixture of anger and pain twisted his features. Everyone turned to stare at me. I awkwardly rubbed my bare arms and ground the tip of my shoe against the cobblestone path.

"Get in the car." Alister opened the door to the backseat.

"Take care of her Craton," I called out as I walked over to the vehicle.

"I always will." He smiled even as his father clapped a heavy hand on the back of his neck and led him into the house.

"This is ridiculous," Marley sneered at me before putting on her black sunglasses. "The amount of risk being taken for you is more than I will accept. Get her back to the city. I'll deal with her there." Marley walked to the second car in line and slid into the backseat.

The convoy began to move. Alister climbed in next to me and slammed the door shut behind him. The tinted window between the passenger and driver was rolled all the way up. We were alone in a sealed box. He sat angrily glaring at me.

"I won't apologize." I returned his glare. "I would never have missed her wedding. I am sorry you are upset and I'm sorry you went through all this unnecessary trouble to give me a ride back."

"Unnecessary?" Alister growled. The intensity in his eyes caused me to scoot closer to the door. "Do you know what could have happened to you? Do you know who these people are? They raised you as an orphan to do their bidding in the realm! You of all people should know the kind of danger you put yourself in."

"They also fed me and paid me. Under your government, I don't even exist. I'm not sure who I should be more afraid of," I lashed back.

"We can change that," he said through clenched teeth.

"Then why haven't you?"

"Because I don't make the policies right now. One day I will."

"Yeah and your policy maker right now is a bitch. I'm still not convinced it is safer on your side."

"No harm will ever come to you when I am here."

I smacked my palm against the leather bench seat. "I am so sick of everyone thinking they need to protect me now that I'm an adult. I've made it this far in life without your help. I am fine on my own."

"Are you?" he smirked. "Because it seems like you make dumb and rash decisions with no concern for the consequences."

"Screw you," I spit. "Every decision I make, I do it out of love."

"That doesn't make them smart ones," Alister chuckled.

"Ugh!" I threw my hands in the air. "And now you are laughing at me."

In one swift motion, he wrapped his arm around my waist and pulled me into his lap. The vehicle bounced along the rocky road. I gasped as he reached his other hand up to the back of my head, lowering me down to kiss him. The intensity and suddenness of the moment left me wanting and disorientated. He took his hand from my waist and slid it down the thin material of my dress.

"You'll take your punishment without complaint," he commanded hoarsely against my lips.

"Is this my punishment?" I stared challengingly into his eyes.

"The president will make some sort of demand for breaking the law. Take the punishment so we can move past this," he said.

"You are out of your freaking mind!" I scrambled out of his arms and back to my seat.

"I was hoping you'd make that decision out of love," he grinned. "But I guess not."

The blood pumped into my cheeks. "Love and lust are two different things." I turned to face out the window, staring at the landscape silently for the rest of the drive back to the city.

Chapter 18

∞

The driver opened the door in front of an old stone building with pillars reaching high up to the arching roof.

"We're not going to the professor's house," I anxiously whispered to Alister as he stepped out behind me.

"No." His face was cold and stern.

I wanted to reach for his hand and beg him to be playful again, but I knew it was my fault he was acting this way. *Sometimes apologies are more important than pride.* I made the mental note to remember that next time.

The line of vehicles from the convoy sat parked on the street. Men and women in their serious looking suits shot me annoyed glares as I looked at them. I kept my head down and followed Alister into the building.

I owe a lot of apologies, I sighed to myself.

Our shoes clicking against the stone floors echoed through the hall. I followed Alister into a wide and open office where Marley waited behind a grand desk.

"Close the door Charles," she commanded to the bald man who never left her side. The sound of the heavy latch clicking behind me caused me to jump. "Come here, Fawn," Marley snarled.

I looked to Alister, but his eyes were downcast as he stepped to the side of the room. Four other men sat on a circular sofa in the opposite corner. I inhaled deeply through my nose as I walked to the center to stand in front of everyone.

"You are a liability to me," Marley's eyes narrowed as she spoke. "And I'd like nothing more than to make you go away."

"I can leave." I narrowed my own eyes despite the fear pounding in my heart. "You won't have to deal with me anymore."

"If it were only that simple," she curled her lip into a cruel smile. "Unfortunately, it's not. This soulmate situation ties you to Alister in ways that I do not understand. While it would be easy to dismiss this as theory, I'm wise enough to know there are elements out of my control here. You will not leave. You will stay and develop your powers in the realm as a matter of national security."

"That makes no sense! There is no nation in the realm. You don't rule there, it's logistically impossible. I refuse to go back, and you can't force me to."

"You really are naive," Marley snorted. "There is more to this than you can comprehend, but yes, I can force you. You will go back. For disobeying an imposed house arrest order," Marley raised her chin as I gasped, "Fawn will have a tracker placed in her body immediately."

"House arrest?" I cried. "No one said anything about house arrest." I turned to find Alister, but he was already rushing to my side.

"Were you not given a direct order to stay at Professor Berlin's residence?" Marley asked coldly.

"Not exactly," I frantically searched my memories in confusion. "It was more like a suggestion to stay low."

"Twist the words however you like," Marely waved with a dismissive hand.

"That's what you are doing right now!" I screamed.

"Auntie stop. This is extreme. You can't force something into her body, and she would need a fair trial for something of this magnitude of service." Alister placed a comforting arm over my shoulders as he stood face to face with Marley.

"I've given enough leniency. You are blinded in this situation. I watched you throw away half of your late father's estate to clear this girl's name." I tensed under his arm as she spoke.

"I allowed you to take the lead on this as you assured me that she would not be an issue and we could trust her. Not only has she caused this whole debacle today, she stands here unstable and unpredictable. She can't control her outbursts and I will need to keep a closer eye on her from this point on."

"You will not." Alister glared at his aunt. "Or the both of us will leave this very minute."

"You know that is not possible," she sneered. "You are the last in the line of Macavays. You know your place. Restrain them," she suddenly commanded the men in the room. I didn't realize they were right behind us until I felt Alister being ripped away.

"Let me go," I screamed as my arms were pinned against my body. I tried to throw my head back against the assailant's face. It hit his broad chest instead.

I twisted my hands and tried to claw with my fingers, anything to wriggle my arms free, while I kicked my legs as hard as I could backwards. Alister punched Charles in the side of his head as two more men tackled his thrashing body to the ground. In the end, we didn't stand a chance.

The man released one of my forearms from his hold and I swung it wildly trying to grab something hard enough to make that jerk let me go. Out of nowhere, a man in a white coat came over carrying a tray of utensils.

I wrenched my neck as I turned to glare at Marley through the hair plastered across my face. "You can't make me go back," I screamed. "Even if you force me to get the tracker, you can't make me go back to the realm."

"One step at a time," she grinned.

"There is too much scar tissue here," the man in white said. "It won't be an easy cut."

"Do it anyway," Marley instructed as she stared at me with cold eyes.

I screamed so loud my ears started ringing. The man sliced the scalpel underneath the thick layer of my skin. The little black disk was slipped into the open cut and I felt its sickly familiar weight. Each stitch sent a shooting pain up my throbbing arm. When the butcher was done, the big man dropped me and walked away.

I curled up on the floor and cradled my arm against my body.

"Are you okay, Fawn?" Alister's voice was raw from screaming too and his head was pressed down against the rug. Charles released his arm and climbed off his back.

"There will be repercussions," he growled at his aunt as he stood up from the floor. "I will make you pay for hurting her."

"Get in control of yourself," Marley commanded. "It was nothing more than a simple cut. It's not like she was seriously injured."

I shakily climbed to my feet and held my arm against my chest. Anger was burning the back of my throat. "And what's your definition of serious? I guess it's not as serious as blowing out Roger's brains, you psychotic bitch."

The room fell eerily quiet as the rage and pain coursed through me. Marley's expression was calm, but I'd seen the hint of fear cause her eyes to shift and I knew I spoke the truth.

"What did you just say?" Alister pushed past the stunned and statue like men as he moved quickly to my side.

"How dare you accuse me of such a thing, you little orphan brat," Marley bitterly spit. "I would never have hurt my running mate and long-time friend." Alister grabbed me by the shoulders and winced when he saw me flinch.

"Fawn, what did you just say?" he asked softly.

"That psycho killed Roger." I glared at Marley. "He told me himself the night that I blew up The Nocere." A range of emotions passed over Alister's face before settling on a tired and determined resolve.

"Marley Macavay, you are under arrest for the murder of Roger Cannon." His cold voice cut through the room like an accusatory knife.

"You are mistaken nephew and I won't have my name tarnished by this street rat," she smirked. "Remove her from my sight." None of the men moved. "I order you to get her out of here," Marley turned to address Charles.

The man looked to Alister. He nodded once and Charles pulled a set of handcuffs off his belt.

"You can't be serious." Marley rolled her eyes as Charles maneuvered her hands behind her back. "What right does he have to accuse me and to order my arrest?"

"Without a running mate, and in the unlikely event of death or detainment, next of kin has always been selected as acting president," the man that had held me said. "You know this Ms. Macavay. It's how your father got his seat."

"I'll see you in court," Marley yelled as she was taken from the room.

My teeth were chattering from the adrenaline drop but Alister looked so pained that I reached out my good arm to comfort him. "What does this mean?" I asked.

"It means I no longer have a choice," he smiled sadly.

"I didn't know that would happen." I held his hand. "I'm so sorry."

"Nothing can be done now." He rubbed his thumb over my knuckles. "I just wish you'd have told me this sooner so it could have been handled another way."

"Roger told me not to tell anyone. I don't know why he told me of all people in the first place. I say the dumbest stuff at the wrong times." I stared pleadingly into Alister's eyes, willing him to forgive me.

"I do," he sighed. "Roger is a very smart man. Are you alright?" He rubbed his free hand over my shoulder. The touch was so calming that I wanted to melt into it, but there were still people in the room.

"I'm fine," I smiled at him. "What are we supposed to do now?"

"I'll get a driver to take you home." Alister motioned to one of the men and he quickly opened the door. "I'm going to have a lot of work to do, but I'll come see you when I can."

Seeing his distant face and troubled walk to the desk made me want to stay, but I'd already caused enough problems for one day. I allowed myself to be escorted to the waiting vehicle.

*

"Stretch your arm out on the counter." I bit my lip as Freida cleaned the stitches and applied a strong-smelling salve to the cut. "I can't believe they did this to you. Didn't I tell you to stay out of trouble?" She glanced nervously at the open door.

The professor had already scolded me and stormed off to his office. I was positive he wasn't listening.

"Thank you for helping me get there. She really needed me. Did Porter wait for long?"

"News travels fast." She tied a loose bandage over the wound. "He heard what happened in the next town over so he knew you wouldn't need a ride."

This small revelation brought me comfort, as did the smell of bubbling stew on the stove. "Will the professor forgive me?"

"Of course he will," Freida sighed. "He is a forgetful man, but his forgiveness is the least of your worries right now. They locked up President Macavay, did they? She is a horrible woman, but I wouldn't want to be on her bad side. And your poor Alister is now the acting president."

"I didn't know this would happen." I pulled my freshly dressed arm to my side. I'd cut the stupid tracker out again, but I'd probably wait until it didn't hurt so much first.

"You wouldn't have known. Our ways are so foreign to you being as that you grew up outside of civilization." Freida went to stir the pot.

"I don't know about that. I think I'm pretty civilized." I pulled a biscuit from the tray when she wasn't looking.

"No manners and no customs. Stealing food like an orphan," Freida laughed with her back still turned to me. I set it back down. "Keep it," she said as she turned around. "You're not bad or wrong, just different is all."

"For as long as I can remember, the Macavays have run the government." She pulled a stool over and sat across the counter from me. "It's always been a relative or a running mate that gets elected, but the name has always been Macavay and it never changes."

"Don't you get to vote? Couldn't you change it if you wanted to?" I asked as I tentatively bit into the bread.

"I always vote for Macavay," she smiled. "They've been taking care of us since the portals were built. No use in mixing things up now."

"I have a feeling Alister doesn't want to be president." I pulled over a napkin to place the half-eaten biscuit on. "And I guess I made it so that he doesn't have a choice."

"That was always going to happen," Freida reassured me. "Better to happen now and get that Marley woman out of the picture. I wonder who he is going to wed." She gave me a knowing look.

"What?" I gulped. "Why does he need to get married?"

"It's a wonder you have lived at all," Freida sighed as she stood up from the stool. "The directive states that all presidents must have a running mate or an heir in case of an incapacitating event. Alister will need to prove he is working on providing an heir in order to rule. He is the last of his line, you know. Poor child." She went to check the stew as my mind raced in a million directions.

Who would he marry? Would he want to marry me? I am not ready to get married. Hell, I don't even know if I want to get married. I mean, yeah, he is hot... but I didn't sign up for this. And who wants to be the president's wife? What would I even do?

"I'm sure he'll choose a running mate," I suggested hopefully.

"Good luck with that," Freida chuckled. "After what has happened with the last two, I can't think of any rational person who would take that job."

Chapter 19

∞

I wrapped the fluffy comforter around me and drowned out the noise of the day with the orchestra notes coming from the earbuds. The pain in my arm had faded to a dull ache thanks to the bittersweet tea Freida gave me. I was bone tired but couldn't turn my brain off.

Vorie waved her ghostly hand in front of my face.

"How long were you sitting there?" I gasped as I turned off the music.

"A while," Vorie laughed. "I was just about to leave."

"I'm glad you didn't." I couldn't control the tears that suddenly filled my eyes and spilled down my cheeks. Vorie soothed me with quiet little shushing hums until my ugly heaving sobs finally subsided.

"What did I just do?" I asked when my voice stopped breaking.

"Exactly what you were supposed to," she smiled reassuringly.

"Stop with the ominous ghostly bullshit," I glared at her. "I need to know why I'm even here. I don't understand why Roger told me that she'd killed him. I don't want to do this anymore. I just keep messing everything up. Since you are this mysterious fortune teller now, can you tell me anything that makes this whole situation better?"

"Everything you are going through now is paving the way to your destiny," she smiled. "Is that helpful?"

"Not at all," I cried.

"Just focus on the present sweetheart, you'll go crazy thinking about the future." Vorie moved to sit beside me on the bed. "Genie's wedding was nice, wasn't it?"

"It was," I sniffed. "I didn't see you there."

"I was watching. That mother in law is a real piece of work."

"That whole family is," I sighed. "But at least we know Craton loves her. Did you know that Fergus is working for his father?"

"I heard," Vorie nodded. "Don't worry about that. It isn't a current problem for you."

"You know what is a problem? Supposedly Alister has to choose a wife right now," I moaned.

"And you don't want to marry him?"

"It's not that. I guess I just never considered myself the marrying type."

"Let him marry someone else then," Vorie shrugged. The weight of her words left a sick feeling in my stomach.

"I'm not sure I would like that very much."

She raised an eyebrow. "No? Well you can't have it both ways. If he has to choose a wife, then it's either you or someone else. Which would you prefer?"

I laid down on my pillow and pulled my knees to my chest as I thought about it. Vorie sat next to me and sang softly until I fell asleep. *I seriously have the best friends in the entire universe.*

*

The birds ruffled their feathers sending the morning dew sprinkling from the tree branches. I stood in the courtyard listening to their music and tending my little garden.

"Come inside, dear," Freida called. "It's time to get you ready."

"Ready for what?" I jumped to my feet. The sun's rays broke over the top of the building and illuminated her frizzy graying hair.

She squinted against the glare. "The first day of the rest of your life, of course."

*

Attendants stood in the hallway outside of my bedroom door. A large white box was carried in and placed on my bed. I removed the lid. Sitting on top of the tissue paper was a single orchid branch with delicate pink flowers.

Great. He is planning to pick out my clothes for everything, I sighed to myself. *I'll have to talk to him about that.*

Inside the box was a simple black pencil skirt and a silk almond colored blouse. Once I was dressed, the attendants yanked my hair from my head as they brushed, twisted, and pinned. I tried to send the makeup artist away, but she pleaded with me so kindly that I gave in to a light dusting. Thankfully, the heels they brought were sensible, so I didn't break my neck coming down the stairs.

"You look very grown up," Professor Berlin said as he extended his arm and escorted me to the waiting sedan.

"You seem less angry," I smiled at him. "Does this mean I'm forgiven."

"Yes," the professor sighed. "You might as well be, we still have many training sessions to go."

"I'm afraid I haven't learned anything," I laughed.

"Oh, but I have." He opened the door. "And you've learned more than you think you did."

*

I wasn't exactly sure what was about to happen. The professor said it was a ceremony. Freida called it a coronation. They promised they would both be in attendance. I knew I wasn't wearing a wedding dress, so at least I had some time to accept that idea, and I knew I was going to see Alister.

That thought made me giddy and I blushed even though there was no one in the vehicle to notice.

The sedan came to a stop in front of the stone building where Marley had ordered the tracker to be placed back in my arm. I gently brushed my fingers over the wound underneath the silk shirt. *It still really freaking hurt.*

The car door was pulled open out of my hands. Alister stood there on the sidewalk smiling at me.

"How are you little deer?" he asked in his smoky, sultry tone.

"I'm well. How are you?" I waited patiently for him to step aside so I could climb out.

"Better now." He motioned for me to slide over. After he sat down next to me, the driver pulled back onto the road.

"Where are we going?" I asked.

"There is an event we need to attend. I'll be sworn in as president and I'll need to make an announcement."

"I see." I turned to look out the window and took a steadying breath. "Is this it then? Is this where you have to pick a wife?"

"They told you about that?" Alister sighed as I nodded. "I see. And what do you think about that, little deer?"

"I think you have to do whatever you have to do," I shrugged. "I see no other option."

"And would you agree to marry me?" he chuckled.

"This is no laughing matter." I crossed my arms as I glared at him. "Was that you asking me? Because it was a horrible performance. But yes. As a matter of duty, and because I got you into this mess, I will agree to marry you."

"I guess it's good that I'm not asking," he smiled playfully. My jaw dropped. *What the hell is that supposed to mean?* The vehicle came to a stop.

"Come on." Alister held out his hand. "We are here already. We can discuss this later."

*

The crowd that gathered in the open yard beneath the stage consisted of more people gathered in one place than I'd ever seen in my life. The blur of faces staring up at us was overwhelming. Thankfully, Alister held my hand and I clung to the comforting yet electric touch as he led me up the stage steps. A woman in a blue suit directed me to stand slightly to the right of the podium.

Alister winked at me before turning to address the crowd. I felt the sticky cool sweat form on my palms as I tried hard to focus on what he was saying. He seemed so calm and collected, so sure of himself, as he eased the crowd's fears with promises of a better and more unified nation.

It was hard to hear him over the cheers and the thudding of my heartbeat in my ears. I forced myself to raise my chin anyway, standing tall beside him. If this was to be my destiny, my future role as the president's wife, I might as well look the part.

"And now for the announcement you've all been waiting for," Alister spoke slowly into the microphone as he glanced back to me. I stood frozen to the spot.

No way in hell is he going to announce our marriage without even asking me first! My brain was screaming but my face stayed stoic. Maybe I'd learned something from these people after all.

"I will be choosing a running mate."

There was a sudden quiet among the crowd, ears open in anticipation. I looked to Alister in confusion and all at once I saw Professor Berlin laughing silently as he shook his head in the front row.

"Miss Fawn Vita will be my second in command," Alister told the waiting citizens. The woman in blue ushered me forward to stand beside him at the podium. My eyes widened as I stared at the side of his face.

"What are you doing?" I whispered to him. The sound of the clapping and cheers drowned out my words.

"Making it so you never have to worry," Alister said through his perfect grinned aimed at the crowd. My thoughts were racing as I tried to process it all.

I mirrored his smile and looked at the people. "This isn't a good idea."

"It's the best one I have."

I felt as though we were speaking in each other's heads. Our unflinching smiles and lips never moved.

"Where'd you get the name Vita? I don't have a last name."

He raised my hand up high in the air as the people continued their applause. "It means life." He squeezed my hand in his. "I thought it would suit you."

Preorder the next book in this series today:

https://www.amazon.com/Other-Side-Haunting-Dystopian-Tale-ebook/dp/B089T98MFY/

The Other Side: A Haunting Dystopian Tale book 3 Releases July 21, 2020

Before you go…

I honestly hate this begging part, but if you have a moment could you please consider leaving your honest review of this book? Indie authors can't survive without word of mouth referrals and reviews from readers like you.

Thanks for reading!

Follow the author on Facebook

www.facebook.com/heathercarsonauthor

Instagram

www.instagram.com/heathercarsonauthor

TikTok @heathercarsonauthor

Make sure to sign up for the mailing list to get your free short story "Katrina's Story" a prelude to the Project Dandelion series

www.heatherkcarson.com

Other works by Heather Carson

Sent to a fallout shelter to survive a nuclear catastrophe, a group of teenagers are the last hope for humanity. Can they survive living with one another first?

Get the *Project Dandelion* series, now in one convenient box set

https://www.amazon.com/Project-Dandelion-Books-Heather-Carson-ebook/dp/B088J6Z9Q7/

Or see that the readers are saying about this YA post-apocalyptic series, book 1-

https://www.amazon.com/Project-Dandelion-Heather-Carson-ebook/dp/B07TLF8HN7/